THE
ESSENTIAL
PUBERTY
GUIDE
FOR
GIRLS

A Complete Resource for Tweens to Understand Their Changing Bodies, Handle Emotions, Cultivate Healthy Habits, And Grow with Confidence and Grace

By

ELI SPARK

Disclaimer Notice

This book is independently published for educational and entertainment purposes. The information is accurate and reliable but not guaranteed. It aims to help readers understand the subject better with self-help activities and exercises. It is not a substitute for professional advice. Consult a qualified expert for legal, financial, or psychological guidance.

By reading, you agree that the author is not responsible for any damages from using this information, including omissions or errors. You are responsible for your own decisions and actions.

Kindle ISBN: 978-1-917358-08-8

Paperback ISBN: 978-1-917358-09-5

Hardcover ISBN: 978-1-917358-10-1

About the Author

Hi there! I'm Eli Spark, and I've spent a lot of time helping girls like you understand what's happening as you grow up. My goal is to create a fun and safe space where you can learn about your body without feeling embarrassed or worried.

Going through puberty can sometimes feel weird and confusing, but it can also be exciting and make you feel more confident! I want you to know that everything you're experiencing is completely normal. Let's explore this journey together and turn those awkward moments into fun and empowering ones. You're not alone. I'm here to guide you!

A Necessary Note from the Author

The puberty years may seem like a time of changes in your body, but they actually begin in your brain. Most girls start getting ready for puberty when they are eight to twelve years old. This is when their brain starts sending hormones to their bodies to get them ready. Remember that you will begin puberty at the right time for your body. You shouldn't expect to start growing at a certain age or grade because every girl's body is different. You also will grow at a different time and pace than your friends or classmates. Some girls mature early, and some mature late. You might hit puberty around the same time your mom did, but that's not specified. My elder sister was almost four years younger than I was when she got her period, but my younger sister got hers at the same age as me. It's okay if you're not at the same stage as your sister, mom or friends. No one else has the same fingerprints as you and no other girl will go through puberty like you. That's a good thing. You are unique.

Table of Contents

Introduction:
Welcome to Puberty Book

You've already read enough introductions, so let's jump into the good stuff! Imagine having a big sister who's been through it all and is here to share her stories and secrets with you. That's what this book is all about.

When I was your age, I had so many questions about things like breast size, periods, and even crushes. Sometimes I felt too shy to ask my parents or older sister. I remember the first time I noticed changes in my body, I was confused and a little scared. I wished I had a book like this to turn to for answers and advice.

So, I wrote this book for you, filled with everything I learned the hard way. Inside, you'll find fun facts, stories from other girls, and even some of my diary entries from when I was a preteen.

Whether you're curious about eating habits, dealing with awkward moments, or understanding your feelings, this book has got you covered. Let's explore this journey together, and I promise, it's going to be an adventure!

I interviewed my peers to find out what they wished they knew before or during puberty. The answers I received were truly insightful and should be included in this book.

1. "It's okay and a beautiful phase of life."
2. "Everything is temporary, so live in the moment."
3. "The world doesn't change just because you have changed."
4. "Embrace your changing body with confidence."
5. "It's okay; even celebrities get periods."
6. "When you know that your world has crumbled down, and now is the time to give up on your life and mourn about it, wait patiently for 2-3 days; everything will be alright. They are just hormones playing with you. Or maybe you just want to eat an ice-cream."
7. "It's awesome to become a woman. All feminine and classy!"
8. "There is nothing to be afraid of when you are growing up."
9. "That having extra painful periods is not normal, and you don't have to bear it all the time. Life is not harsh on you specifically; everyone goes through this and eating won't make you fat."
10. "I wish I knew that body hair is here to stay and I have to remove it - Pubic hair, specifically."

The life of a girl is filled with physical challenges. This is an undeniable truth that half of the global population knows but hardly speaks about. Something is spurting, sprouting, blooming, or blossoming at almost every step of a girl's development. Many metaphors involve the garden.

Can you believe it? Your body had this incredible ability to detect when it was time to start maturing. Consider this. No aircraft can take flight without a pilot, and a computer, no matter how powerful, requires activation from a human. However, your reproductive system is brilliant and can determine the precise steps needed to transform you into a woman. *What a fantastic, ideal creation of anatomy!*

If you want to know what to anticipate, how it works, and how it could feel during puberty, this book is for you. You will also learn how to combat harmful beliefs and practices related to periods. You can return to this book and read sections later if you need to know more details than what is presented here.

Take it easy on yourself and your body for the next few years. There will be highs and lows as you navigate the journey of growing up. However, you can enjoy yourself while this book guides you through it all. Are you prepared? How about we begin?

Part 1
Out of Shadows:
Understanding Puberty

No matter when or where you were born, puberty is the same for everyone. Just like it was for your parents, the changes happening in your body guide the entire process.

Francine Pascal

Not sure about all the changes your body is undergoing—inside and outside? You are not the only one. Having the right knowledge about what is happening in your body will help you, whether you are at the beginning of this process or have already experienced some of the body changes described in this book. This will help make it easier and perhaps less demanding.

Puberty occurs whether or not you feel ready for it, but as your teachers have most likely already said to you many (many) times, knowledge is power. Knowing what will happen within your body will enable you to prepare for it. While surprises might be appropriate for birthdays, they are not entertaining when discussing the significant changes associated with puberty.

But what exactly is puberty?

The process your body goes through to move from childhood to adulthood is known as puberty. Many of the internal developments and changes are not visible from the outside, while others are evident. Often, when girls consider puberty or growing older, or what adults refer to as "becoming a woman," they picture the monthly cycle. Though one clear sign of puberty is the beginning of your period, there is much more involved than just that. Dealing with Puberty is best done without following a schedule. Try hard to avoid evaluating yourself against the behavior of your pals. While some girls start puberty as early as eight years old, others start far later.

Being earlier or later than your friends doesn't make you strange; puberty is a very personal process, and your body changes when it is ready.

The First Signs of Puberty

Ammy's mom came to pick her up from school. Ammy quickly climbed into the car and buckled up. She said with a frown, "Ow! It hurts a lot!". "What's wrong, honey?" her mom asked as she looked at Ammy in the rearview mirror. She said, "The seatbelt strap hurts. It hurts a lot in my chest." In the evening, Ammy was bathing when she felt dark hair under her arms. She yelled, "MOM!" in shock. Ammy's mom ran up the stairs and looked shocked when she saw her in the tub.

Ammy's mom helped her comb her curly hair after bathing. Ammy looked at her mom with confused eyes and said, "Mom, I've noticed many different things going on with my body lately." Her mom asked her nicely, "What have you noticed?"

Ammy thought momentarily and said, "Well, I'm one of the tallest people in my class this year." Also, my chest hurts and has bumps on it. I'm also getting hair under my arms, which none of my friends have. Her chin shook a little. Mom hugged Ammy and put her arms around her. She answered gently, "I've seen these changes too. It looks like you are starting to go through puberty. This means your body begins to change and grow into an adult body. Everyone goes through these changes, so don't worry about them." Ammy's eyes got bigger. "Being a teen? Wow!! When did you start going through puberty?" Amy asked curiously.

After some thought, her mom said, "I think I was ten. Puberty begins at a different age for each person. We are going to see your doctor next week for your yearly

13

checkup. Let's talk to her about the changes you've seen. She will know a lot and be able to answer any questions you may have." Ammy smiled and gave her mom another hug, feeling better. Ammy's best friend, Sera, came over to play the next day. Ammy started laughing hard while the other girls dressed up and started crying suddenly. "What's wrong?" It made Sera wonder. "I believed we were having fun."

Ammy wiped a tear off her face and said, "We are—I am. I don't understand why I feel so many different things. I'm thrilled one minute and sad the next. It's not clear at all." Sera reached out and grabbed Ammy's hand. She was sorry for her friend and all the different feelings she was having.

As you read the story of Ammy, did you find something relatable? Something that is happening with you as well? If yes, then these are the first and foremost signs of hitting puberty.

- Breast growth
- Pubic hair
- Mood swings

Your Body's Changing: What to Expect

acne   oily hair   underarm hair

The changes usually happen in this order. It takes about four to six years to go from having a little girl's body to having a full-on young woman's body.

1. **The Secret Part:** This can happen at any time between the ages of 8 and 11. Inside your body, glands and organs get more extensive and release hormones. You might get taller, and your hands and feet might get bigger.

2. **The Breast Stage:** Most girls get their breast buds between the ages of 8 and 12. Breast buds are the first thing that show up. There are hard lumps under each nipple. Often, one comes before the other. The nipples will push out after a few months or even years, and your breasts will begin to grow. You might also have a growth spurt as you get bigger and taller.

3. **The Stage of Pubic Hair:** This usually takes place after the "growing breasts" stage. It's also normal for about one in five girls to get pubic hair before they have any changes in their breasts. The first hair is thin and straight.

4. **The Menstrual Stage:** Most girls get their first period about a year or two after the first sign of breast change. Doctors call this Menarche (pronounced menark). Many girls get it between 9 and 15, but it doesn't matter when they get it. Most call it between the ages of 12 and 13.

The hair in your **pubic area** typically gets a little thicker, darker, and curlier as you age. You're still getting taller, and even though you can't see it, your vagina is getting bigger, which is good if you want to use tampons during your period. You may also notice a small amount of clear or white fluid on your underwear. This is vaginal fluid.

The **hair growth** under the arms starts between the ages of 9 and 14, but most often, this can happen between 10 and 12. Also, hair starts to grow in the triangle-shaped area under the breasts.

At this point, the **nipple area** will also start to form. Also, your ovaries release an egg occasionally, but probably not every month yet.

By the time you're 16, your breasts and body hair growth are "complete," and you're at or near adult height. You get your period every month, and about halfway between periods, your ovaries usually release an egg and this process is called ovulation.

The Science Behind Puberty

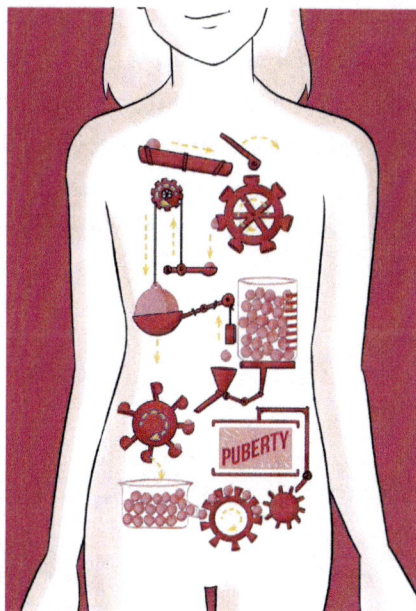

We need to talk about chain reactions right now. This is going to be too simple, so don't worry. Your body part that starts the chain reactions of puberty is the ovaries. A part of your brain called the hypothalamus is where it all begins. A hormone is released by the brain, which tells the pituitary gland to release another hormone. This hormone wakes up the sleepy ovaries.

As you grow up, your ovaries are like light bulbs that have been turned down very, very low. They're there, but they're not doing much. Then, when you hit puberty, they turn up the noise a bit and get to work. When I say 'get to work,' I mean that those hormones are no slow panda but a fast cheetah now. The ovaries produce hormones like estrogen and progesterone. These hormones move through the body and tell different parts of the body to do other things, like increasing breast size, hair growth, hip width, and periods. It's a really complicated chain of events.

Why are there so many changes? You're becoming a grownup and moving on to a new part of your life. Girls who have been through it before know how it can feel like you're in the middle of a storm.

You start to notice little changes in your body just when you think you're getting good at being a kid. After a while, you begin to feel different about yourself, your family, and your friends. Also, the adults around you might start to say that you're "on your way to becoming a woman," even though no one asked you if you were done being a girl yet.

Let's discuss these changes and hormones a bit more clearly on the next page but first it's time to smile a little :)

Let's Laugh

Puberty is a massive software update that takes a few years to complete.

Hormones: Your Body's Messengers

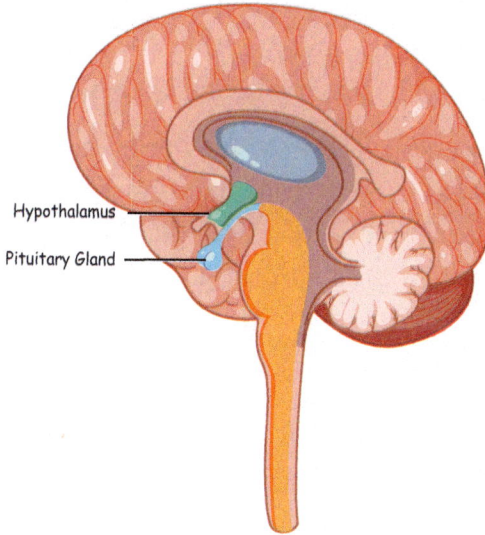

Hypothalamus

Pituitary Gland

Chemistry is what keeps our brains and bodies going. Hormones are chemicals that control many body functions, such as operating systems that control periods. Hormones are very important to our life! These chemicals are made by endocrine glands, which are part of the endocrine system. Your body changes in obvious ways during puberty. For example, you get your back molar teeth and grow taller. The chemicals are to blame for these changes. Hormones also tell your reproductive systems that they must grow to their full adult size. Many chemicals control the steps, and it depends on your gender and age when they happen. Because of the glands and chemicals that are here, periods are possible.

The hypothalamus, a structure in the brain, releases the hormone GnRH, which sends messages to the pituitary gland, which then releases the hormones FSH and LH. Some hormones make it easier for eggs to come out of the ovaries. The ovaries produce two different hormones, estrogen and progesterone. Estrogen and progesterone tell the cervix what mucus to make at different times during the monthly cycle. Along with making the endometrium thicker, estrogen helps egg cells mature until they are ready to leave the ovary. After that, each ovary stops producing eggs and begins producing progesterone.

When progesterone levels drop, the uterus must lose its lining. Along with the eggs, the adrenal glands (one above each kidney) also make progesterone. Along with the testes (part of the male reproductive system), the adrenal glands and ovaries release a small amount of testosterone. This hormone alters mood, energy, muscles, and desire.

Let's now explore how hormones regulate our emotions and how to manage them.

Understanding and Managing Your Emotions

Do you remember how Ammy's emotions were all over the place?

Emotions and thoughts may flood your mind. Difficulty or confusion could set in. You get angry or hurt easily, even with those closest to you. Sometimes, you don't understand why you're grumpy. You can laugh for one second and cry the next. This is a perfectly normal reaction to changes in hormone levels. Discuss your emotions with someone if you've been consistently sad for longer than a week. Someone should help you if you're feeling down.

When your mind is occupied by different thoughts, try not to dwell on them. Having a little "me time" can be helpful for you while going through puberty to sort out your feelings. If you're in a bad mood, why not curl up in your pajamas and listen to your favorite music? You may prefer reading a book or painting. When life gets hectic with school, friends, and family, it's important to remember to do what makes you happy.

Emotional imbalances are a normal part of growing up, so try not to be too hard on yourself if you experience them. We're all imperfect. This is especially true during puberty. A few days of sadness shouldn't be taken as an indication that you'll always feel down. You don't have to be constantly angry, even if you have been yelling a lot lately. Keep in mind that troublesome hormones and the brain are to blame.

In the next few pages, we will be discussing how your body changes in puberty.

A Note to Parents

When it comes to puberty, kids who know what to expect usually have a much better time than kids who aren't ready. Please take a moment to remember what it was like to go through puberty. Have talked to your kid about growing up and what to expect? You are one of the lucky few if you did! Many of us don't remember the best parts of going through puberty. Our parents never talked to us about going through puberty. Sometimes, they did, but it was just one big talk we didn't understand. This meant that we didn't know what to expect during puberty. We now know kids will handle puberty better knowing what to expect. They need to know what will change about their bodies, why it will change, and how to take care of their new bodies. You're not the only one who wants their child to have much better puberty years than you did. So, what are the most important things we should tell kids?

- The puberty years are when your body changes from a child's to an adult's.
- There are changes in both the body and the mind.
- All kids go through puberty, and it's normal.
- There are slow changes.
- Puberty happens to all kids, whether they are male or female. Puberty years begin at different times for different kids.
- Everyone is unique.
- Your body is already set up to give you the body you were meant to have.
- You can't change this.

Part 2
Forces of Nature: Morphology of You

Going through puberty as a young girl is so confusing. This monster invades your body, changes things and makes things grow, and no one tells you what's going on.

Katherine Isabelle

Are the shoes you bought last month too small? If your trousers, which are almost brand new, no longer fit you, you're likely experiencing your first growth spurt during puberty.

Puberty years are a time when everyone grows. You're getting bigger and gaining weight faster than you used to. This time when you grow very quickly is called a growth spurt. Each girl starts at a different age. It happens at different rates for each girl, but they all experience significant growth during this time. This growth spurt typically lasts for a few years. Afterward, the growth rate slows down and eventually stops.

In this chapter, we'll discuss several aspects of the puberty growth spurt. Two key components are the height spurt and the weight spurt. However, the growth spurt during puberty affects more than just your height and weight.

This could make your face and body look very different from how they did before puberty. You might look more like an adult than a child!

There are many ways to grow and develop, but living well and working out are two of the most important. A lot of young girls don't do either, though. These girls don't do enough movement or eat foods that give them the necessary vitamins and minerals. For young girls, this can prove awful for their bones. When you hit puberty, your bones become strong for the rest of your life.

Let's see how puberty changes your morphology.

Growing Taller and Stronger

Each year, a girl grows about two and a half inches longer than she did the year before. Growth speeds up when the height spurt starts.

A girl may grow almost twice as fast as a boy, growing about four inches yearly. During puberty, a girl's height usually grows by nine inches. You might grow more or less than this because everyone is different. Most of the time, the growth spurt lasts for three years. During your teens, you may slowly get taller or have a few short growth spurts or one long one. Some girls grow several centimeters in a year. Girls usually grow the most quickly when they are 12 or 13. Your growth rate slows down by the time you get your first period.

You'll only grow one or two inches a year after that.

First, your hands and feet get bigger and then your arms and legs. Finally, your back gets longer. It gets stronger due to your muscles. These changes happen slowly for some girls and quickly for others. Changing quickly can affect you. It might make you feel off balance and a bit awkward or clumsy as you get used to the new you. But don't worry, you'll get used to it soon.

Girls, when puberty starts, you need to let go of your unrealistic ideas about what's normal and healthy when it comes to being fat. It's normal for you to gain both strength and fat. It's part of growing up. Young women and girls (say, 16 years old and up) who are fit and beautiful should have 25 to 30 per cent of their body fat. Fat is not a bad word. It doesn't mean too fat; it means the right amount of fat.

You need to have at least 22% of your body weight in fat and about 17% body fat to start having your periods. Generally, a ten-year-old girl has 10 to 15 per cent more body fat than a boy of the same age. Women are 10 to 30 per cent fatter than men of their age. The girly fat stuffing is mostly around your breasts, hips, and stomachs. It's there to help your body protect the reproductive organs.

Changes in Breasts and Hips

Phases of Breast Development

Phase 1

Phase 2

Phase 3

Phase 4

Phase 5

One thing that happens during puberty is that your hips get bigger. This is because the hip grows, and fat starts building up in this area. When you hit puberty, hormones like estrogen are released, which can cause your hips to get wider.

Some girls can't wait for their breasts to grow. Some girls may feel like they have got their bugs too early and may even feel weird or embarrassed around other girls of their age who aren't as fully grown. But despite these feelings and the fact that most girls your age can't develop breasts until a certain age, there is a lot of diversity in the puberty process.

Some girls develop their breasts as early as nine years old. Some girls might not get breasts until they are almost 14 years old. Being different from your friends might make you feel bad about having breasts that grow later or earlier than they do.

After all, who wants to be different?

Your chest is mostly flat when you're a child. You start to develop "breast buds" around the age of 9. This saying has always made me laugh, and when I first read about it, I imagined my breasts as flowers. Don't worry, though. You're not going to get roses or flowers to grow on your chest. These buds are different from the flower buds. There's no need to worry if you start developing breast buds earlier or later. Most girls do it between the ages of seven and twelve. Your breasts will grow at the right time for your body, just like all the other changes that happen during puberty. It will be clear that your breast buds are growing when you feel something behind your nipples pushing them out a little. Your nipples will stay mostly flat, though.

Breast growth usually happens in five steps. Some girls skip steps, so not all girls will go through all five phases.

Phase one: Before Puberty

As a child, you don't have breasts because your body hasn't started making estrogen or developing mammary glands yet. There may be very, very early signs of puberty going on inside the body, but there are no visible signs.

Phase Two: Breast Buds

Your mammary glands will start to form between the ages of 8 and 11. By that time, estrogen will be moving through your body. Your areola and nipples will get bigger and start to stick out, making small buds that might feel like lumps under your nipples. There is a chance that one "bud" will appear before the other, so don't worry if you see one nipple sticking out farther than the other.

Phase Three: More Fat

During this time, fat will start to build up around your breast glands. You might notice that your breasts are becoming pointy and decide that it's time to start wearing a bra. The size and shape of these fat deposits, where they form, and how they change over time will determine the overall size and shape of your breasts.

Phase Four: Development Continues

Some girls skip right over stage four and never even go through it. Some girls might stop here. If you are in stage four, your nipple and areola will keep growing and may form a mound. This will make your breasts look pointy or cone-shaped.

Phase Five: Mature Breasts

By the time you reach stage five, your breasts are usually fully developed. They might change a bit in shape and size if you gain or lose weight, have a baby, or breastfeed. But for the most part, they're the breasts you'll have for life. Treat them kindly, care for them, and appreciate them — they'll be with you for a long time.

Finding Clothes That Fit and Feel Good

Huge amounts of money are spent every year on ads that tell you to buy the best bras. In general, bras and underwear cost more if they are fancier and slip on better. But the main reason for wearing a bra is easy: to keep your breasts from moving around and bouncing around, especially when you're working out hard. When breasts bounce, it can hurt, be annoying, or make people stare. A bra made of metal would be the only thing that could completely stop all bouncing, which would feel awkward and uncomfortable. That's why bras are made to reduce bouncing instead of stopping it completely.

Around the time they reach phase three of breast growth, most girls start wearing bras. The soft material of a bra can help protect your sensitive skin and nipples as your breasts grow. It can also support your growing breasts. When your breasts start to show through your clothes, a bra can also help cover them up.

Many girls only need to wear a bra when they're active, like during workouts, dancing, or playing sports. If bouncing doesn't bother you, you might not need to wear one all the time.

But if it does bother you, then it's best to buy your first bra in person, even though there are a lot of websites that sell them. This way, you can make sure that they fit and feel good. There are many bras in stores made specifically for teens and girls who are just starting puberty. While pants and T-shirts usually come in small, medium, and large sizes, bra sizes are determined by measuring around your rib cage and the size of your bust.

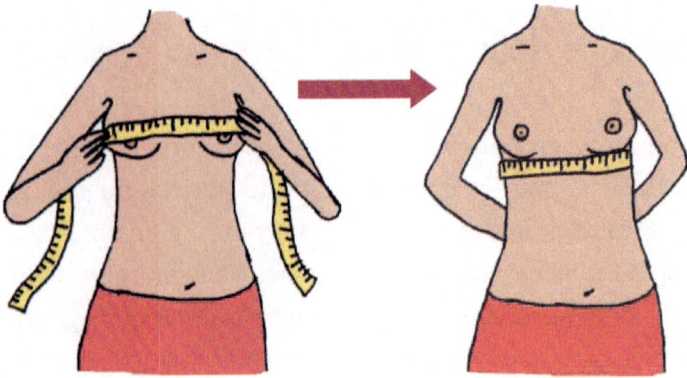

You can measure yourself, but it's better to have a professional do it. All you need is a tape measure with inches on it. For every bra size, there is an even number for the band size (28, 30, 32, 34, 36, etc.) and a letter for the cup size (A, B, C, D, and then double letters for bigger breasts).

Tips for Measuring

Take a measuring tape with inch marks and wrap it around the point where your breasts are widest. This will give you your bust line. There should be enough space for your finger to fit between the tape measure and your skin. Check out the number where the tape measure ends. This is how big your bust is.

To find out what size band you need:

1. Lift your arms off of your body and put the tape measure around your middle, just below your breasts.
2. Check out the number where the tape measure ends.
3. Round up to the next even number if it's an odd number.

In this case, a size 34 will fit someone who is 33 inches around. If the number is even, that's your band size. You can also try the next size up to see which feels better. It's time for math! Use your math skills to find the difference between your band size and shoulder size.

The Right Fit

Besides making sure the bra fits well, you should also wear the right bra for different activities, so that you are comfortable and your breasts stay in place. Wearing soccer cleats to dance class and ski boots to school are two things you would never do. The same goes for bras! When you don't have the right support, your breasts can get stiff and painful, which is not fun at all.

Training Bra

T-Shirt Bra

Sports Bra

Underwire Bra

Padded Bra

Bra Alternative

Below, I'm explaining some bra types for you.

1. Training Bra

Training bras are for girls who are just starting to develop, but you're not really training for anything! They are made of soft materials and come in smaller cup sizes, which is great for getting used to wearing a bra. Sometimes, training bras are also called "bralettes."

2. T-Shirt Bra

You won't be able to see any lines under your T-shirt because T-shirt bras don't have lines or seams in the cups. Most of the time, these bras are made of cotton, which lets air flow through them.

3. Sports Bra

You guessed it, this bra is for playing sports! You can also use it whenever you need a little extra help. It's made to keep your breasts in place while you work out, whether you're playing basketball, dancing, or running around with your friends. Most sports bras are made of spandex or another very stretchy material, and they don't have clasps, so you pull them over your head. A lot of girls think that sports bras are the most comfy. If you agree, then you should wear them all the time. You don't have to keep them for sports time only!

4. Bra with Wires

An underwire bra has real U-shaped wires under each cup to give you extra support. When you wear an underwire bra, make sure the wires lie flat against your rib cage so that the bra fits right.

5. Padded or Lined Bra

For extra support, you can get a bra with either light or thick padding. As women age, some choose to wear thick bras to make them look better.

You can wear a camisole (a top with little straps) made of soft fabric instead of a bra. You can also wear a crop top or a vest top. Some tops now have two layers of fabric under the breasts, and some even have a small elastic "shelf" underneath to make it less likely that nipples and jiggles will show.

> ## Health Tip:
> Do not wear a bra at night. Let your breasts rest for a while.

If your bras are made of silk, lace, or even stretched cotton, it's a good idea to wash them separately from your other clothes to make them last longer. You should also hang your bras to dry because the machine can damage stretched fabrics, bend underwire in underwire bras, and snag delicate fabrics. The heat can even make bras shrink! When it comes to pants, you can wear any style that makes you feel good.

Serra was in sixth grade when she wore her first bra. She was fussing with the straps in class one day. A boy saw her and loudly said, "I just saw your bra strap! You have a bra on!" She felt ashamed. She wasn't even telling her friends she was wearing a bra yet! Some of the classmates laughed, but she just said, "So what? Do you want to wear one?" and went back to take notes. She really felt like crying inside because she was so ashamed. Riya, her friend, came up to her at lunch break and said, "Don't worry. I have started wearing a bra too." When she smiled, Serra felt relieved knowing she wasn't the only one feeling that way. It didn't matter that they hadn't talked about getting bras—they were both going through the same thing.

Never forget that you are not alone during your puberty years, even if things feel scary or awkward.

Let's Laugh

I looked like a potato until I reached puberty.

Skincare Basics for Clean and Healthy Skin

Girls who go through puberty may worry a lot about their face because of one word: acne. Acne is also known as pimples or "zits." The tone of your skin and how likely it is to get scars, freckles, pimples, dimples, or lines depend on your ancestors in the family tree. Cosmetic labels often try to convince people they need special products by talking about different skin "types." Sometimes, this approach works.

These are the different kinds of skin:

- **Oily Skin,** sometimes called "teenage," "troubled," or "problem" skin, is shiny and may have bigger pores than usual.

- **Dry Skin** lacks any oil or moisture, so it's more likely to flake, get rough, dry spots, or get eczema.

- **Normal Skin** shows no issues with oiliness or dryness (though this may not be common).

- **Combination Skin** means that your face has a mix of oily, normal, or dry spots.

When skin is sensitive, it usually reacts with a rash or redness to cosmetic chemicals, heat, allergens, and alcohol. For sensitive skin, it's best to use skincare products that are fragrance-free and labeled "hypoallergenic" (unlikely to cause an allergic reaction).

Problem: Girls can easily get spots and blackheads, especially those with oily skin. If you have oily skin, choose products labeled "oil-free" or "non-comedogenic," as they won't clog your pores.

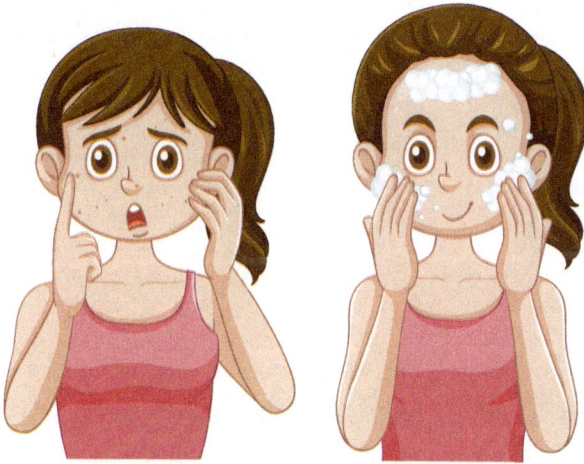

Health Tip:

Do not pick at your pimples. This irritates your skin and can cause scars.

You know that almost everyone gets pimples on their face during puberty, but when they appear, it's not easy to handle them. When bacteria (germs) and dead skin cells mix with oil that gets stuck in your pores, you get a pimple. You can't completely avoid getting acne. Changing hormone levels in your body are partly to blame for the extra oil on your skin. But there are some things you can do to make your skin look and feel better.

1. **Cleanse:** Wash your face every morning and night. Some people wash their face with soap and water, but soap can dry out your skin because it removes the oils that your skin needs. To get rid of the oil on your face, you should buy a soft cleanser that doesn't work like soap and is made just for the face, not a body wash that doesn't have oil in it.

2. **Moisturize:** People use moisturizers to keep their skin from drying out too much. Your skin can get too dry if you wash it too much, take very hot baths, shave or wax, spend a lot of time in the sun or swimming, or spend most of your time in buildings with cold or hot air. That can trick your body into making more oil, which can lead to clogs and spots. A lot of girls don't need to moisturize their face or body, especially those who live in hot places or drink a lot of water and get enough oils from nuts and fish.

3. **Scrub:** When you rub coffee beans mixed with honey on your skin or use any other scrub, they remove dead skin cells because they have rough, crunchy "beads" in them. Most teens don't need to use a scrub on their face because washing with a face wash or cleanser twice a day should be sufficient to remove dead skin cells. If you scrub too hard, your skin could become irritated and flaky. Also, avoid using a facial scrub on your face more than once a week or using a body scrub on your face.

Do not use any skin care product unless prescribed by the dermatologist. Your skin needs healthy food and air to glow. Follow the rule: cleanse, scrub and moisturize.

Healthy Skin Tips

Eating well reflects on your face. To improve digestion and the absorption of nutrients, drink plenty of water. This also keeps your body and face hydrated, though additional water does not prevent spots. The more you work out, the more blood flows to your face, which helps heal and clean up any skin problems. If you don't want to get lines or dull skin, don't smoke or be around people who smoke.

(We will discuss it all in part 6 of the book)

Managing Hair Growth: What You Need to Know

oily hair   clean hair

Girls can find it hard to take care of their hair because there are so many hairstyles to pick from. There are some things that you should always do, no matter what style of hair you have.

Hairstyling

1. Scrub. Clean. Say it again. Your hair may become thicker as you go through puberty. That's those annoying hormones behind it again! If you're very busy or if your hair gets very oily, you might need to wash it every day.

2. Use hair care items that are made for your hair type. Different hair types need different grooming tools. Read the labels or ask someone at the cosmetic shop for help. The place where you get your hair cut can also give you some ideas. But keep in mind that hair products bought at salons are typically more expensive than those bought elsewhere.

3. Heat isn't very good for your hair. Hair can get damaged when you use chemicals (like coloring or perms to smooth or curl it) or apply a lot of heat (like blow-drying) on it. This makes it harder to take care of your hair in the long run. Using these methods less often means you won't need as many special conditioning products for your hair.

4. It would help if you wash your hair every night. Using hair products to style your hair can be fun, but you should wash them before bed. This is especially true for things that are made of wax, like some kinds of oils. Washing your hair before bed prevents it from being covered in product all night, so you don't wake up with hair that looks like it belongs in a horror movie.

Body Hair

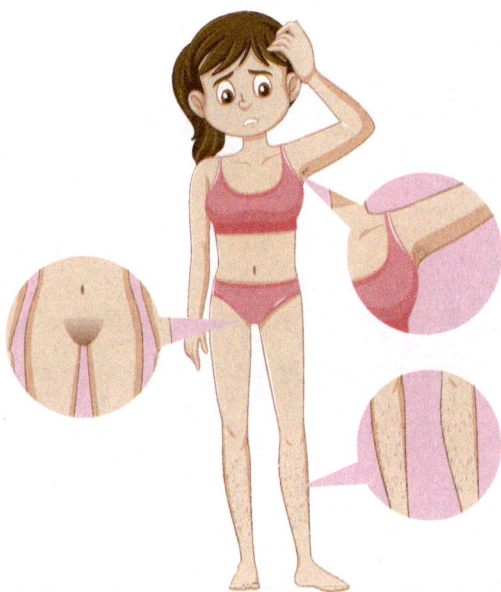

Body Hair? What is even happening???

Everybody has hair on their bodies. Many times, people with fair skin don't have as much body hair as people with darker skin. Different groups of people, like Asians, have less body hair than others. Some girls, like those with Italian, Greek, Turkish, or Arabic roots, have more body hair than others. If you have a lot of facial hair, it could mean that you have a hormone problem, like polycystic ovaries, which can be treated. If you think it's getting out of hand, you should see a doctor. Girls who are starving themselves and don't have enough body fat may get downy hair on their arms and back. This is their body's way of trying to stay warm.

You can get rid of body hair and pubic hair in a number of different ways. To live a healthy, clean life, you need to get rid of your pubic hair and armpit sprouting hair. If you don't, they can itch, smell, and give germs a place to grow, which will be very embarrassing for you.

Unexpected Body hair

Your wrists (below the elbow).

The snail trail: You may grow a line of darker hair from the area around your pubic mound up to your belly button. On the top lip, every woman has a small mustache. You might get hair here and there around your nipples as you age. Having a little hair around your private parts is typical.

Some Ways to Remove Body Hair

Shaving

Girls and women usually shave their underarms and the part of their legs below the knee. This is because these areas are easy to get to and stand out the most when it's warm outside. Shaving costs less than other ways, but hair grows back very quickly. You can use an electric shaver, which costs more, or a razor, which works best with warm water and shaving cream. No matter what "they" say, shaving doesn't change how fast, slowly, thickly, or darkly the hair grows back. Because the hair is not cut from roots, new growth feels rougher and sharper. Shaving every day, even if it only takes ten minutes, adds up to more than an hour a week, which is more than three whole days a year! This is why many people only shave the day before a leg-show-off event.

Plucking, Waxing, and Threading Hair

Waxing pulls the hair out from the roots. That's why it doesn't grow back as quickly as when it's cut or shaved. Hot or cold wax is applied to the area, and then a piece of cloth is put over the wax and quickly pulled off, removing the hair with it. You can either do this yourself at home by following the directions on a product from the pharmacy or grocery store or pay money to have a professional do it at a beauty center. Most people put wax on their legs, sideburns, eyebrows, and upper lip. If you wax anywhere on your face, especially on your upper lip, you could get pimples or rashes. There is no need to put hot wax near your eyes. Instead, go to a salon. Waxing can be painful, especially in the beginning, and you should do it every three weeks to two months at the very least.

You can remove single hairs by plucking them with tweezers or threading them, pulling them out by the roots. When you thread, you wind a cotton thread around the hair to pull it out. When you pull out hair by the root, you may hurt the hair shaft. This can make hair grow back less quickly or cause hair to get tangled in the thread.

Creams

Creams are the easiest to use when it comes to removing unwanted hair. Depilatories are strong chemical creams or liquids that dissolve hair so it can be wiped off. When used incorrectly, creams can still irritate and cause rashes. Before you use them for the first time, you should do a patch test. Please do not use depilatories on your private parts without doing a patch test first, and never use them on other sensitive areas of your body, like around your eyes, mouth, or open wounds.

shaver	cream	wax	epilator	laser
1-3 days	3-7 days	2-4 weeks	3-4 weeks	forever

When I first started getting hair in my armpits, it was a big deal for me. My friend told me that she had taken her dad's razor and that she shaved her legs, arms, and armpits! It took me a long time to figure out how to ask my mom for a razor. Then, one day, while my parents and I were sitting on the couch, I raised my arm and told my mom, "Hey, look! I have armpit hair. May I have a razor?" I tried to sound like I had just noticed it, which is what I did. On the inside, I was going crazy. After a few days, I came home to find a razor on my bed.

- Kelly

From the age of ten to sixteen, I competed in swimming events. Around the age of 12, when I started getting hair down there, I noticed that the older girls shaved their bikini areas. I used shaving cream and a blade to get rid of enough of it so it wouldn't show. It's not something I remember ever talking to my mom about; I just learned it from watching all the other girls.

- Anna

A Note to Parents

The shape of your child's body will also start to change. It will get bigger and curvier. Their hips will get bigger, and they'll start to see a stomach. As their bodies start to store fat, they will get heavier. This weight gain can happen quickly within one to two years or it can happen more slowly over three to four years.

Some girls and young adults worry that they need to lose the weight they gain during puberty. It is important to know that during puberty, your child should gain weight. The jumps in height and weight sometimes happen at different times during puberty. They might feel like they're gaining weight sometimes, but then they'll grow quickly, and the fat will spread out to fit their new height.

Part 3

The First Womanhood: Menstruation Time

No one else sees it. No one else wants to. Only she can see the beauty in her blood.

Nikki Tajiri

Take a look around. Every woman you see has had her period. And if she hasn't already, she's probably starting, ending, or about to start her period again. Even though it may seem silly, knowing that we're all in this together makes you strong. The most interesting thing about this is that you don't know which women around you have their period.

Every girl gets periods, but it's something that isn't visible to others. The world doesn't always understand when or what is happening.

These words might not seem very helpful when you're in the bathroom and dealing with thick, bloody discharge from your vagina, but I'm here to tell you that it's all normal and even pretty cool. Maybe one day, you'll change the way you think about your period. You might find that it helps you remember that your body works as it should. It may seem strange when you're dealing with the mess, shame, and even cost of your period, but older women who have gone through menopause say that they miss it when it's over. That's because your body has a kind of clock that tells you when to menstruate every month unless you're pregnant. It tracks when you first start getting your period until you stop getting it. It might be too much to take in or get out.

This part might be a little messy, but I think every girl should know how her body works. Your body and you will always be together. Every time you talk to each other, you'll feel better.

Understanding Your Menstrual Cycle

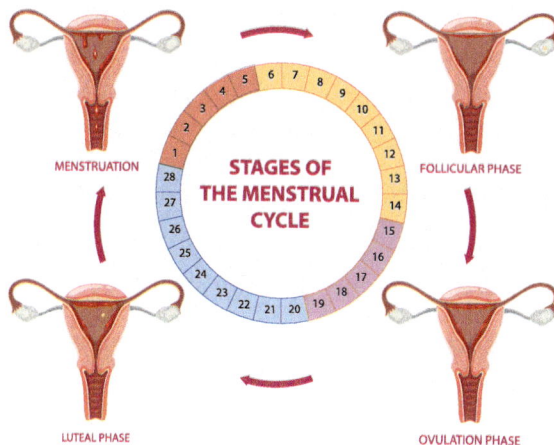

It's a big deal to get your period as you need to be able to have a baby one day. It's a physical sign that you are becoming a woman. Your body is preparing for this change. That's why your mum or health teacher might tell you that you become a woman when you get your period. When the ovary stops making hormones, the lining of the uterus starts to break down, which is when menstruation begins. This drop also makes your hormone levels drop. The pituitary gland works again when the hormones drop below a certain amount. It sends a hormone to the ovary again, making about twenty more ova form. The ova make more significant amounts of estrogen as they grow. Once more, the lining of the uterus starts to get thicker because estrogen levels go up.

When the amount of estrogen reaches its highest point, another mature egg is released from the ovary. If the egg isn't fertilized, the lining falls off, and a new period starts. This is the start of the menstrual cycle again. This whole circle keeps going around and around. It is called a menstrual cycle when it happens more than once.

You might get your period on the first day of one month and again on the first day of the following month. This perfect cycle might be rare in the next few years of having your period. But as you age, you'll probably notice all the signs and symptoms of what's happening during the month. Most women have their periods every 28 days, but yours may be a few days longer or shorter.

Each woman has a different cycle length. It changes from one woman to the next during her cycle. An adult woman's monthly cycle lasts about twenty-one to thirty-five days.

The average is about 28 days, but not many women have periods that occur every 28 days every month.

A woman may have her period for seven days in a month. The next cycle may last 29 days. After that, the cycle could last thirty days. Each of us has our own style. Different people are more or less consistent. Most of the time, women between the ages of twenty and forty have the most normal periods. During your period, thick clumps of blood called clots may form. When you change positions after sitting or lying down for a while, it is more likely that you will see clots. Clots are most likely to discharge when you first wake up. There's no need to worry about clots as long as the flow rate is average.

When girls get their period for the first time, they often worry that they have pooped in their pants by accident. Most of the time, the fluid from your first period is brown. Remember that if you look in your pants and see something brown, it's usually your period.

Period blood can be dark pink, bright red, dark red, brown, or a mix of those colors. These colors are all fine. The color might also change from one period to the next or even from one day during your period to the next. If the color remains consistent, that's also perfectly normal.

Recognizing Signs of Your First Period

This will be the first time you will see period blood on your pants. You won't feel any blood coming out of your vagina usually.

You might feel what doctors call "breast tenderness" before your period. It's possible that your chest hurts or feels full and heavy before your period.

Changes in hormones bring on these feelings and are often signs of your period. You may get pimples or notice your skin getting oilier or drier at some point in your cycle. These things always take place at the exact time. When you know what's normal for you, you can tell where you are in your cycle or remember to do your skincare routine.

You can tell when your period is coming after a while. In the days before your period, you may feel teary, clumsy, and grumpy, and experience fuller breasts, leg pain, and bloating. This is called premenstrual syndrome (PMS) or sometimes premenstrual tension (PMT). Don't worry; that's not because your body is holding on to a lot of blood; it's just other fluids.

Symptoms of periods can be very different for each person. You should get help if your PMS makes it hard to enjoy life.

Preparing for Your First Period

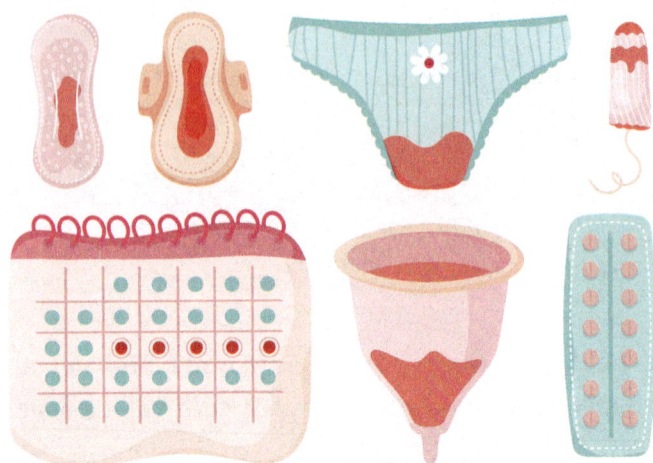

You cannot really decide when you are going to have your first period, but you can be prepared by keeping in mind the first signs of your period. Some girls let all their friends know when they get their period.

Health Tip:

Start carrying a pad with you, whenever you're away from home.

Some girls only tell their best friends. Some girls may only tell their mum and aunts or choose to keep it mostly secret. Whatever makes you feel good is what you should do.

Remember that it's your private information, and you don't have to give it to anyone, even if they ask. Also, no one can tell that you've started your period just by looking at you.

You might feel like your period is an exclamation point for the first few years! Your first periods can be irregular. They may start and stop and may not go as planned when you're sick or worried. You're not alone. Most girls will have regular periods by the end of their first year or within a few months.

Let's Laugh

Whatever they can do, you can do while bleeding.

Essential Items for Your Period Kit

Period pads and tampons, also called "feminine hygiene products," are small, single-use items used to soak up period blood. They can be found at most corner stores, convenience stores, grocery stores and pharmacies.

Some girls don't feel ready to use tampons at first because they are pushed up inside the vagina. Instead, they try pads first. When you leave the house, always have a period bag on hand.

Next, I'll explain the different types of items you can use for your periods.

1. **Pads:** There are curves at the ends of a pad, also called a sanitary napkin. The back has a sticky strip that you stick to the inside of the crotch of your underwear (the part between your legs). Some pads now have flaps or "wings" on the sides that stick to your underwear and help keep the pad in place. If you have a heavy period, you may need to change your pad up to three times a day. It can be hard to do this on a school bus trip, but you should change pads every eight hours.

2. **Tampons:** A tampon is a tightly rolled piece of absorbent material. It has a rounded end that makes it easier to slide into the vagina and a string that is firmly attached to the other end. To pull it out, you gently pull on the string. A tampon is cleaner than a pad because it soaks up the blood before it leaves your body. A tampon can be worn while swimming, but a pad can't be worn. You should use only one at a time. Tampons should be changed after every two hours during heavy flow, just like pads. No tampon should be worn all night or for more than four hours at a time.

3. **Menstrual Cups:** You can use a menstrual cup to catch your blood if you have your period. It fits inside your vagina and, with the help of your muscles, acts like a stopper with a weak suction cup effect. You use the small stalk or ring on the bottom to take it off. During your period, you need to empty your menstrual cup often. You might have to empty it several times during the day, but you can leave it in for 6 to 8 hours.

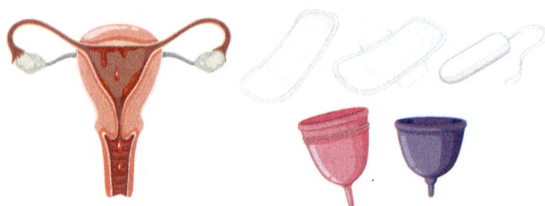

You'll figure out what you need in your period kit on your own soon, but here are some ideas:

- Pads and tampons.
- Wet wipes to clean yourself.
- Cotton for the heavy flow.
- Two or three small, folded-up plastic or brown-paper bags for putting used pads or tampons in before you throw them away (Some pads come in their bags, which you can use to roll up used pads before throwing them away).
- An extra pair of underwear. This is in case you get blood on your current underwear.

The day you use something from your kit, like a pad, don't forget to replace it with a new one in your kit.

Dealing with PMS and Cramps

Many times, when women complain about having their period, it's because of the cramps that come with it. There may be girls out there who have never had cramps before, or perhaps I just haven't met any of them at that time of the month. Period cramps are different for each girl and will probably change throughout her life. In the years after your period, cramps are more likely to hurt. Some girls have minor cramps, while others have terrible cramps that can make it hard to move.

Let's start by talking about why you have cramps. What you already know is that your period happens when the lining of your uterus falls off.

The contraction of the uterus causes the pain, so this can happen. In medical terms, cramps are called dysmenorrhea. They are caused by prostaglandins, which are chemicals that make your uterus tighten.

Depending on how bad the cramps are, there are different ways to deal with them. Sometimes, putting a hot water bottle on your lower stomach can help. You might be surprised to learn that exercise also helps.

I'm being honest here. Most of the time, walking or swimming is the fastest way to get rid of bad cramps. I won't lie — they can get terrible. If they get bad, you can ask your parents for an ibuprofen or another medicine. After having your period for a few years and getting to know it better, you'll probably be able to tell when you'll get cramps: the day before, on the first day, or in the middle of your period. You can then use one of the above ways to deal with them.

But what if your cramps are so bad that nothing helps?

It is possible to do this. Some women's periods hurt a lot. If any of these women have period cramps that are very painful and make it hard for them to do things, they should see a doctor.

Sometimes, agonizing cramps can be a sign of a deeper problem. But sometimes it's just cramps. Your doctor can help you figure it out and give you ways to handle it. Know this is real, and don't hesitate to ask for help.

Ways to fight PMS?

You need help getting rid of bloating and water buildup. Eat fewer salty foods and drink a lot of water. Check every package to see if salt or sodium is high on the list of ingredients like Coffee, tea, chocolate, cola, energy drinks, processed meat and other foods rich in sodium. Wearing a firm crop top or bra can help your more prominent, sensitive breasts feel better. To keep your energy up between meals, snack on healthy foods. This doesn't mean a Snickers bar; it means a handful of nuts and some fruit or vegetables.

Medical herbalists may recommend a variety of herbal, vitamin, and mineral products to help with the general symptoms. Vitamin B6, magnesium, vitamin E, and evening primrose oil are often given the most attention.

When I woke up in the morning, there was blood on my sheets. I was shy, worried, and maybe even excited. I asked my mom to check on me in my room. It's funny because I used to study religion every morning with my grandfather, but girls don't have to touch the religious book on their period days, so I was glad to skip the morning routine. I still remember the look on my grandfather's face when my mom told him that I was having my period. He looked worried and almost sad. I took that look on his face to mean, "My grandchild is all grown up now." When I got to school that day, I couldn't wait to tell my friends that I was finally an adult.

- Susan

I quickly changed clothes in my room because my mom wanted to go shopping. I took off my yellow shorts and saw blood! I knew about periods; my best friend got hers when she was 9. But it was still a surprise. I stood still and yelled for my mom. I was sitting on the toilet when she ran upstairs, took one look, and left me there. Ten minutes later, she returned with a bunch of pads ranging in size from pretty big to really huge. I was shocked! I'm thankful I was with my mom at home, though, because she told me everything would be okay.

- Kris

A Note to Parents

Puberty is not always the nightmare that it seems to be. Different people handle this time in their lives in various ways. One thing you should know for sure is that kids have a lot less trouble with puberty when they ask questions. If things are more accessible and understandable for your child, they will be easier for you, too!

- Having trouble figuring out who they are and having questions about themselves are common feelings that your child may have during puberty.
- Changes in mood, anger, and sadness.
- Getting a little more sleep than usual.
- They want to be bigger and are in a hurry to grow up.
- A desire for more freedom and privacy.
- Their friends and other people's views are becoming more important to them than their family.
- Being more worried or interested.

Part 4
The Scary Superstitions: Facts, Myths, and Taboos

We live in a world where it is easy and comfortable to wear it, but miserable to talk about it!

Shriya

Periods make women feel a lot of different emotions. When you do or say something that is considered taboo, you might feel bad about yourself if you get caught doing it. This makes you believe in all the taboos. Some people may avoid you or the taboo subject in many small ways might make you feel bad or in trouble.

When you feel humiliated, you think you're wrong for doing something that other people think is embarrassing or wrong. If you have been mean or hurtful to someone, you might feel bad about yourself, which is awful. Embarrassment about your period can make you feel bad about yourself and make you think that your body or you are wrong. That's not right!

Some cultures around the world have always thought that periods are good and important, while others have disagreed on the issue. Sadly, most cultures still have detesting ideas about it. Girls haven't really felt like they owned their periods for a long time because of these rules that were either not said or spoken.

Even though most of these rules no longer apply, shame is still a powerful feeling. You shouldn't feel wrong about the way your body works, but it's hard to stop feeling that way while the views are still there. Look around. Once those views disappear, people who have periods will feel less embarrassed about them and more confident about other things.

The good news is that people are beginning to change their minds. It's becoming increasingly common for everyone to agree that periods are a normal part of a healthy body and that we should all talk about them and help individuals who are having issues with them. Being different has taken a long time and is still happening slowly. Let's speed things up so we can start feeling better now. Let's look at how these attitudes have been affecting us for a long time.

Exploring Global Puberty Superstitions

Some of the global superstitions associated with periods are:

1. **Stay out of the kitchen:** It is pretty standard for women not to be allowed in the kitchen while food is being cooked, both in rural areas and in some cities of India. A lot of the time, they depend on family members to bring them food. Because of this, most rural women don't get enough protein. Many societies believe that women are dirty when they have their periods, which leads to this cruel practice.

2. **Avoid touching women who are menstruating:** As another unfair practice, this keeps up the idea that women who are on their period are dirty. People in communities and families need to understand that menstruation is a normal biological cycle and not a bad thing.

3. **Do not wash your hair:** The myth says that women should wait to wash their hair for at least two days after their period. This probably comes from the time when baths had to be taken outside in streams, which made it difficult to take a bath while bleeding. But in this day and age, it's just one of those silly things people say.

4. **Stay out of the house for three days:** In many countries, a lot of girls and women have their periods in an animal shed or a shed they have built outside their homes. The practice of being by yourself is known as chhaupadi, and it originated in Nepal. The myth of Chhaupadi stems from the belief that menstruation women are impure and bring misfortune to the community. It's crucial to realize, though, that women who live alone run the risk of being assaulted sexually, attacked by animals, and left out in the cold.

5. **Don't go to religious places:** This idea stems from the notion that bleeding women are 'dirty' and therefore they should avoid religious events and places. Women are also instructed to stay in their rooms if possible and are not allowed to attend religious meetings.

6. **Only pads should be used.** This cannot be true. Using tampons is often linked to the risk of having problems with the hymen. Having no idea that the hymen could break even with sports or other activities and that having a hymen does not mean you are a virgin.

7. **Do not water any plants or go near the Tulsi plant:** The Tulsi plant is thought to be holy, so girls who are on their periods are not allowed to touch it. During this time, they can't even walk around plants in some places. The story says that if you do that, the plant will die.

8. **Period Blood is magical or destructive:** Some parts of the world believe that women throw their "used" rags or pads at a road crossing to curse or harm other people. It is said that anyone who steps on this thrown rag or pad will get the evil eye or black magic.

Let's Laugh

The sharks will eat you if you swim while menstruating.

Myths vs. Facts: What's True?

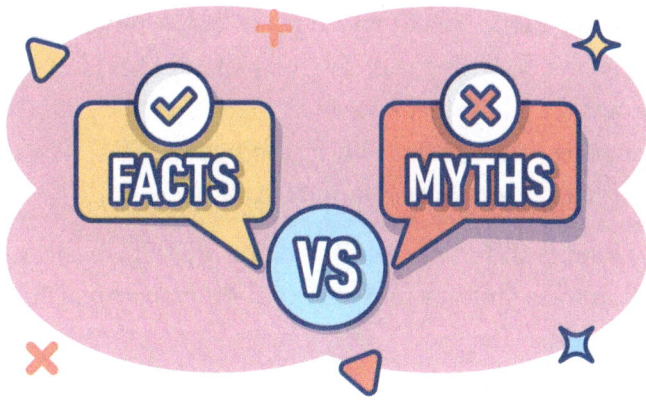

Let's talk about some of the most common myths about menstrual health and what the truth is about each one.

Myth #1:

Period pain isn't excruciating.

Fact: It's easy to think that period pain is just an exaggeration if you've never had one. Certain women are lucky enough to be able to walk through their periods like they're in a sanitary pad commercial, like dancing in a field of flowers while wearing a pretty white dress.

But for some people, periods are so bad that they have to take time off of work or school to relax. This kind of pain and difficulty is called dysmenorrhea in medical terms, and about 80% of women experience some form of it at some point in their lives. Imagine sharp pains, constant pricking in your legs and backs, and cramps. These signs may be a little different from one period to the next, but you get the point.

Myth #2:

Period blood is gross.

Fact: Period blood is not the type of body fluid that is being rejected by the body or the body's way of getting rid of toxins. It's a more advanced form of vaginal discharge—it contains some blood, uterine tissue, mucus lining, and germs in it. Always wash your hands after touching it, and be careful with it.

Period blood is different from the blood that flows through your veins. It moves quickly out of your body because it contains mucus and other fluids.

Myth #3:

You have PMS all in your head.

Fact: When you are on your period, have you ever felt really upset about other girls? Or did you feel like the world was ending because someone ate the last piece of cake you saved? You're not by yourself. No, it's not in your head either! One in four women have PMS, which stands for "Premenstrual Syndrome." PMS usually starts a week or two before your period and is marked by headaches, bloating, and, you guessed it, bad moods. Because your estrogen and progesterone levels drop so quickly at this time of the month, it may feel like your hormones are on a roller coaster.

You might not be able to control your hormones, but you can control them by doing things like eating well, staying away from stress, and getting enough rest and sleep. See your doctor if the symptoms are too bad. They can help you figure out what changes you can make to your lifestyle or medicines you should take.

Myth #4:

When you have your period, you should stay away from certain things.

Fact: As already discussed, periods can be challenging, but that doesn't mean you can curl up in a ball and eat chips all day if you don't have dysmenorrhea, an accident, or any other illness. Period pain, like cramps, headaches, and back pain, can get better with exercise and over-the-counter pain killers. Also, a little exercise might give you the energy boost and feel-good chemicals you need.

Just remember to pay attention to your body, drink water, and rest when you need to. You can work out while you're on your period by doing yoga, Pilates, light running, or weight training. Remember only to work out when it makes you feel good!

Myth #5:

Each period should only last one week every month.

Fact: To begin with, it's important to understand that a woman's period is not the same as her monthly cycle. The exact time a woman bleeds is called her menstrual cycle, which spans from the beginning of one period to the start of the next.

The average length of a woman's monthly cycle is 28 days, but many people think it lasts longer. The cycle of periods lasts between 29 to 35 days for some women, while it may last less than 24 days for others.

Not being able to get pregnant causes your hormone levels to drop, which makes your uterus lose its lining. The next day is the start of your actual period, which usually lasts three to seven days. But what if you get your period only a few months or if it goes away for more than 90 days? You don't need to sound the warning just yet, though. When a woman gets her period, things like travel, changing weight, age, stress, low body fat, lifestyle, emotions, and medicine may all change your period date.

Myth #6:

When you have your period, you can't swim.

Fact: There is an urban legend that says if you swim while you're on your period, sharks will come and attack you. There's no scientific proof that women on their period are more likely to be attacked by sharks. No one wants to end up in a scene from Jaws for real. The other common myth is that swimming while you have your period makes the water dirty or puts you at risk of getting an illness. Again, this is not true because period blood does not contain the same germs as pee or feces which could make the pool dirty. If you want to avoid making a mess and don't want to deal with putting a pad under your bikini, a tampon or a menstrual cup is a better choice. And remember to clean up thoroughly before and after getting in the water, just like you would when you're not in the water.

Myth #7:

There is only one best way (using cloth instead of pads, tampons, and menstrual cups) to deal with your period.

Fact: There are many ways to deal with your period, depending on your preferences. Pads are easy to find, menstrual cups are affordable, and tampons are flexible. You might not agree with ads or even your friends, but there isn't just one way to handle your period that works perfectly. Actually, every tool and method has its pros and cons. It depends on your skills, interests, and way of life. For beginners, organic pads are great for people with sensitive skin or who want something more comfortable and better for the earth. People who bleed a lot could use period underwear or pads, and people who are always on the go could use menstrual cups. In the end, you need to do your research and choose the option that works best for you.

Cultural Traditions around Puberty

1. **Brazil:** When girls in the Amazonian Tikuna group get their first period, they live in private rooms in their families' homes for three months to a year. The Tikuna live in Brazil, Colombia, and Peru. Girls spend this time with other girls from their tribe and learn about their history, music, and values. It is an essential event for all girls who are becoming women. At the end of this time, there is a party, and the girls are welcomed back into the society.

2. **Fiji:** When girls get their first period, some groups set up a special mat for them to use. The girls learn how important this event is in these places. While the girls are on their fourth day of their period, which is called "tundra," their families celebrate by having a party.

3. **South India:** Groups hold a half-sari event or a ceremony called Ritusuddhi or Ritu Kala Samskara to honor a girl's first period. She is becoming an adult now. The girl wears a traditional outfit called Langa Voni, which is a skirt and sari. It is usually given as a gift. A half-sari is another name for it. Girls who are old enough to understand what they need to do for their families and society can make changes to traditions at this event.

4. **Japan:** When a girl in Japan gets her period for the first time, her family might eat a traditional food called sekihan. It is made of sticky rice and adzuki beans. The dish's red color means happiness and celebration.

5. **North America:** Native American groups in North America hold a ceremony called "The Sunrise Ceremony" to honor girls who have reached puberty. Girls from the tribe take part in different rituals during the event and give and receive gifts. The girls dress in cultural clothes that symbolize womanhood. They also have a feast to celebrate. Native Americans in North America see the transition from childhood to adulthood as an important time in their children's lives. To mark this important event, they hold a number of coming-of-age ceremonies that show their support for traditional and community values.

Breaking the Taboos

A taboo is a religious or social rule that says you can't do or be around certain people, places, or things in a certain way. When people follow firm views, they are not allowed to do certain things. These are called taboos. But taboos are there to make sure that societies work the way that certain groups think they should.

One common taboo regarding periods presents the idea that women are dirty, unclean, or sinful when they are bleeding. To keep the water in a shared bathroom from getting dirty, some women are told not to touch or wash their private parts while they are on their periods. Women and girls are denied a basic right: the right to their health and cleanliness. This is because of taboos and false beliefs.

Keep in mind that people in the past didn't understand how the body worked.

They also had different ideas about what was good and evil, right and wrong, and clean and dirty. People who were menstruating were often not allowed to do certain things, like cooking, farming, or growing food, because it was thought that menstrual blood was so strong that it could poison or spoil food. We now know that periods are good, but these negative messages that keep the old taboos alive are still around in some parts of the world.

There are a lot of people who believe that if you have to talk about periods, you should call them something else and whisper. When they talk about something that makes people feel bad, they often use a term. A euphemism is a word or term that people use instead of one that might make someone feel bad. A lot of euphemisms are used to talk about periods. It's also known as a visitor, a friend, or Aunt Flo (*sounds like "flow", doesn't it?*).

Some women make jokes about their underwear color, while others say "I got it" as a secret code. Some code words, like "the curse," support the idea that periods are dirty or dangerous. The word "period" is a code word! It stands for "period of menstruation." People thought that no one should get their periods because they couldn't talk about them. Women were told to hide their period goods and even their period blood. This is why blue liquid is often used instead of red in ads for period goods. But remember, period blood and leaks don't need to be hidden, and no one should feel ashamed about experiencing them. No matter what you use, accidents can happen, like stains on your clothes. You don't have to hide the fact that you get periods or how you handle them.

Building Confidence through Knowledge

It's helpful to be able to talk about these things with someone who remembers this time in her life. Talking with friends can also be helpful. You can find a lot of beneficial information about how your body and life are changing in books like this one and on the internet. It would help if you always keep in mind that you know the most about your own life.

Spend some time thinking about your identity and goals. Stop the hustle for a while. It is difficult to understand what's going on in your life when you're always busy.

Don't worry about why someone doesn't like you. Not everyone has to like you. It's enough if only a few people like you. You can get rid of mean people and meet new ones. There are people out there who think and like the same things you do. Perhaps you'll have to wait until you finish school or move out. There is a bigger world out there than your school, neighborhood, or town, and you have a place in it.

A Note to Parents

Some tribes like to celebrate their child's first period to mark the phase toward becoming an adult. Realizing that your child is leaving their childhood behind can help them a lot. When planning a party or event for your child's first period, consider its significance within your family. There are many ways to do this, but you need to make sure your child is pleased with it. Please pay attention to what they want to do to have fun.

Here are some ideas:

- Have dinner together as a family.
- Have lunch by yourself with your child.
- Give them a card, flowers, or candies.
- Write them a letter in which you share your hopes and dreams for them.
- Make a party box with things they might need during their period, like period products, new underwear, a heat pack, cookies, essential oils, and so on.
- Give them a new book to write in.

Part 5

The Emotional Enigma: Psychological Health

Puberty for a girl is like floating down a broadening river into an open sea.

G. Stanley Hall

Puberty years are a time of change, that's what you should remember from this book so far. Big change. We've mostly talked about changes in the body, but during puberty, a lot of mental growth also takes place. The person you are changing into is smarter and more aware of the world around you. That is, you start to think differently. As you get older, your emotions and thoughts also change. This means that you probably think about things in your life more.

You could feel like a helium bubble floating in the wind one minute and full of life, happy, and excited the next. Sometime after a few minutes, you may feel like your balloon has lost all of its air. You could be tired or sad, and you could even want to cry. What's going on? You have cried before, but never after a good day at school or when nothing was wrong.

The truth is that your thoughts become clear when you hit puberty. Because of all the hormones in your body! Life is full of stress. You can surely get rid of it. You need to figure out how to deal with the things that stress you out. In the same way that different things make different girls worried, different girls deal with stress in different ways. Some things, like the fact that the school fair was moved back a week, might not bother you, but your best friend might start to freak out because of it.

While I was going through puberty, I had times when I was really upset. It was weird that sometimes I wanted to cry even though I wasn't sad or upset. When I cried one afternoon, my sister asked me what was wrong. I told her "nothing" because I had no idea why I was crying. It was just "growing pains," she told me as she hugged me.

She meant that growing up is hard on the heart.

You need to declutter your brain from negative thoughts every once in a while. Many changes are happening in your life right now. Sometimes you need to take a break and remember that it's okay to feel sad. You are still you, even with all the ups and downs. You're still the same girl; you're just becoming more of the same girl. Adding to the things you've already done and getting ready for new ones is what growing up is all about.

> When you don't understand why you're feeling so different, know that it's all a part of the process. These changes can be painful, but they are worth it!

Managing Mood Swings

You already know from earlier in this book that hormones control the growth of breasts and pubic hair. During puberty, your hormones act like the sun, providing nutrients and nourishing your body, similar to how the sun nurtures plants for growth. To start, let's review the basics again: Women have eggs, and the hormones estrogen and progesterone are produced by the ovaries. On the other hand, guys have testicles, which make the hormone testosterone.

The body has many more hormones, but these are the ones that matter for puberty.

It's tricky with hormones because they can change your brain and mood too. Only a few studies have directly linked hormones to mood, which is pretty shocking. However, doctors usually agree that hormones can cause mood swings and make you irritable.

The amount of mood swings you experience between the ages of 10 and 18 can skyrocket. Sometimes you're happy to go shopping in shoes, a hairnet, and socks while singing show tunes at the top of your lungs and playfully hitting annoying people with an umbrella, but the next day you might feel really scared and want to hide. It can be so embarrassing to go shopping suddenly or say something out of the blue that you want to move to a different country and live in a tree house for the rest of your life.

Adults can also get moody, but girls during puberty are known for their mood swings because they're different from the time when they were little kids when they were more emotionally stable (except for toddler meltdowns).

Feeling all over the place and ups and downs could be caused by several things.

- You might be cranky because your brain hasn't had enough sleep.

- The chemicals in the brain are not working right, which can happen in teens. They need to be balanced to help you feel calm and happy.

- Teenage hormones are often to blame for mood swings. For example, when girls and women have more estrogen, their brains make more dopamine, which makes people feel better. But when their estrogen levels drop, as they do every month, their dopamine levels drop too, and they may feel less happy all of a sudden.

- Some girls feel flat, tired, grumpy, teary, or nervous right before and during their periods when they have a lot of progesterone in their bodies.

- You think too much about what's wrong with you. Girls during puberty go through a lot of stressful things, and being moody can be a normal reaction to that.

"A little while ago, when I hit puberty, it became harder for me to keep my emotions in check. Now, I get mad or upset sometimes when I'm not even sure what made it happen. I'm aware that I'm more sensitive now than I was before. People in my family call me the mean-ager. Even though I know they're kidding, I get very angry when they say it. It doesn't help that they say it when I have PMS or am in a bad mood, making it hard for me to be anything but angry."

- Julia

Let's Laugh

Cast me in the movie 'Inside Out'. I've got more emotions than they do.

Coping with Anxiety and Stress

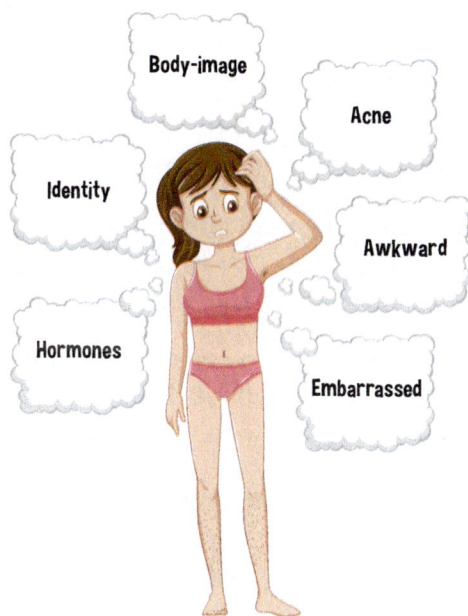

When you feel anxious, you're worried, concerned, or scared about things that might happen. It can lead to panic attacks, which make you feel scared or "frozen." If your worry is too much, you should get help. When you feel stressed, you feel like you can't handle or control all the things you need to do or live up to other people or your standards. The main difference between stress and anxiety is that anxiety involves worry about a specific thing, while stress is related to multiple situations or events.

Anxiety and stress can also affect your body. For example, your heartbeat may increase. You may sweat a lot, have trouble sleeping, and get a lot of colds and infections because your body is too busy dealing with the anxiety or stress to keep up a healthy immune system. Some girls get headaches, stomachaches, or sickness, which means they feel like they might throw up. People often do a lot to avoid things that make them anxious or stressed.

Here are some good ways to deal with worry or anxiety:

- Talk about how you're feeling with your parents, your aunt, a doctor or nurse, a friend's mom, a counselor or teacher, or anyone else you feel safe with. Get some exercise every day; it can help you feel better.

- Leave something (not a valuable vase) like a friend who makes you feel bad, your part-time job, a school subject, or one of the three sports you train for every week.
  Get your mind off of it – Instead of staying home all afternoon and thinking about your worries, go to the movies with your friends or join some activity.

- Think about how you can get out of the stressful or anxious situation and try to keep it from happening again. What could go wrong? (Who can help you with that?)

- Caffeine, which is found in coffee, soda, and "energy" drinks, can make you feel shaky. It will help you deal with things better if you get more sleep.

- A quick and easy way to calm down is to breathe slowly. Take a deep breath in for six counts (or four, if that's easier for you). Hold your breath for a moment, and then try to let it out for six counts. Do it again for about a minute. You should start taking some yoga classes to learn more about the benefits of breathing exercises.

Boosting Your Self-Confidence

When you're sure of yourself, new things happen in your life and you have a more interesting time. Self-confidence is the trust in your abilities. A confident you can handle things in a better way.

You can feel good about your skills, talents, and abilities by following these steps.

- Adopt a straight sitting style. It makes you look more confident.

- Don't hide behind a haircut that covers your face or clothes that are too big for you. Let people know who you are.

- You shouldn't worry about what's in style; wear what you like.

- Wear clothes that are comfortable and won't trip you up or fall off.

- Know that you have a lifetime to get used to your new body, even though it feels strange right now. Keep telling yourself that you will get used to things and be happy "in your skin."

- Take it easy on yourself. If you mess up or do something that makes other people laugh, don't tell yourself you're useless.

- Friend yourself first. If you want to make someone feel better about themselves, what would you say to them? Say it to yourself.

- You are not born to be liked by all the people on earth. There will always be someone who doesn't like you. Avoid such people. Spend time with supportive friends.

- Do things that make you feel proud of yourself. Connect with people who compliment you on your achievements.

Understanding and Expressing Your Emotions

During puberty, it's normal to feel sad or angry. Understanding and dealing with your emotions can help you feel better.

Use your emotions to figure out how to take care of yourself. It might take time to understand what your feelings mean, so be kind to yourself.

- *If you stayed up late the night before, are you feeling sad? You might be tired.*
- *After a long day at school, do you get mad at your little sister? You could be exhausted or stressed.*

When you feel upset, it means something might need to change in your life. If a friend is making you sad, try talking to them about it. Think about what your brain is trying to tell you when you're upset.

Remember to take a deep breath when things get tough. Close your eyes and slowly breathe in and out a few times if you feel down. Fill your lungs before breathing out all the air.

Finding Support: When and How to Ask for Help

When you're upset, it's important to talk to someone you trust. This could be your mom, dad, or another adult you feel comfortable with. Talking about your feelings can help you understand yourself better.

Think about what you would say to a friend who told you they were sad. We are often kinder to others than we are to ourselves. Imagine one of your friends telling you they feel bad about the same things you do. What would you say to them? Use that same kindness when talking to yourself.

According to the research conducted on girls' puberty in 2018, it was found that a lot of girls talked to a lot of different people. About two-thirds of the girls talked to their friends, and one-third talked to both friends and strangers. A quarter of the girls only talked to their dad, while a small group talked to both parents. Girls also talked to God, their sisters and brothers, their aunts and uncles, their cousins, and their elders. Some girls said that they talked to a psychologist, school counselor, favorite teacher, or doctor. Others chatted with online friends, wrote in a journal or blog (but were careful about privacy), or talked to their pets.

Sadly, almost ten percent of girls said they didn't talk to anyone about their problems

Pick someone to talk to, no matter what.

A Note to Parents

Your child should understand from the beginning that going through puberty will not only change their body but also how they feel. This could be helpful to tell your kid these things:

- It's normal to feel all of these new feelings. It's also normal to worry about growing up. Being excited about or in a hurry to grow up is fine. It's also okay not to want to grow up. Sometimes you might even feel like you are going crazy.
- Puberty years are a time for everyone. The way you
- feel will be shared by some of your friends or someone else.
- It can be hard to go through puberty. There are many ways to show strong emotions. Figure out what will work for you, like going for a run or swim, writing in a notebook, or talking to someone.
- Your moods may change, making you sad one minute and happy the next. After a few years, life can be a roller coaster of different feelings.

Part 6
A Sound Body: Keeping Fit

Our body is the only one we've been given, so we need to maintain it; we need to give it the best nutrition.

Trudie Styler

Try not to let your feelings guide what and how much you eat. Instead, pay attention to your brain and body. Know what makes you eat when you're not hungry.

When you're not hungry, you might eat because you're bored, sad, or nervous, you want a "reward" or treat, the food is easy to get, someone else is eating it, or you just want to eat it because it smells good. These situations need something else, not food.

When you're hungry, eat. To lose weight most of the time, you need to let yourself get hungry and then eat until you're full. Use your judgment. Try different amounts to find out what's right for you. Are you really hungry? Do you need a smaller or larger portion right now?

Small shops and fast food places often serve silly-sized meals, like guinea pig-sized muffins and buckets of oily popcorn the size of a car.

Take a chill approach to food. That being said, don't get upset if not every meal is exactly the right amount of everything. Today is not a good day to have to weigh a mushroom.

Try new things. Food isn't just food; it can also be fun! Find new foods to eat and new ways to cook for yourself and your friends. Try new tastes and foods from around the world. It's okay to try something more than once until you get used to it, as your taste buds can change over time.

Try not to make things off-limits. There is no such thing as "bad" or "naughty" food. You'll want a whole block of chocolate if you tell yourself that you can't have it ever. Learn to eat or drink it less often. Try not to eat by yourself or in front of the TV while rushing through your meals. Instead, use meal time to catch up with family or friends.

Eating a Balanced Diet

You need to find and eat good food. You need to eat certain foods at certain times. Here's what you need to know to make sure you don't miss out on good stuff. Federal Health Service (FSA) and the Department of Health say that you should eat five portions of fruits and veggies every day.

That's a total of five full meals, not five separate vegetable meals and five separate fruit meals.

They are full of healthy vitamins, fibers and minerals. It's best to eat a lot of different fruits and vegetables. Eating five bananas all at once doesn't count as separate servings.

It's about half a cup of vegetables, such as peas, carrots, sweetcorn, cabbage, beans, or lentils. It's also about half a pepper, half a zucchini, or two pieces of broccoli. Potatoes don't count because they're a "starchy" food, and neither do chips because they're made in heavy oils and have extra fats that aren't needed.

If you want to eat a lot of different vegetables, try steamed or stir-fried vegetables, homemade soup, salad, or raw vegetable sticks with a dip and a bowl of soup. Frozen vegetables that you "snap," like peas, are better for you than canned vegetables because they keep more of the vitamins and minerals.

In an Asian-style dish, serve vegetables with a splash of low-salt soy sauce. In an Italian-style dish, serve them as pasta sauce, or make a salad sandwich with them. Chopped fresh herbs, garlic, grated lemon peel or lemon juice, and pepper can be used to add flavor. You can have one whole medium-sized fruit like an orange, peach, pear, apple, or banana, or two whole smaller fruits like a kiwi, plum, or orange, or a handful of grapes or berries, or one or two slices of a bigger fruit like a melon, mango, or pineapple.

When you eat veggies, make sure you get a mix of them, like in a fruit salad. It's cheaper and gives you more fiber than juice or shake, which your body needs for better digestive health.

Grain foods have a lot of carbs, which are our most important energy source. They give us the energy we need to move. Carbs are also good for our brains. You might have heard that "low-carb" foods are always the best. Aha! It's not good for you to eat a few carbs, especially when you are a kid.

Our bodies need protein to function well. You can get protein from foods like fish, chicken, duck, lentils, chickpeas, nuts, lean meat, and turkey (without the fatty white parts).

Calcium is good for your bones as they grow, and dairy foods have a lot of it. They are made from milk from moo cows, and you should eat three servings of milk, cheese, or yogurt every day. It's equal to a glass of milk, two thin slices of cheese, or a small tub of yogurt.

Eating healthy fats and oils is important to maintain balanced hormones, healthy skin and hair, and aid in the absorption of vitamins. Choose healthy fats found in oils like olive oil, fish oil, and almond oil.

Try not to drink sugary soft drinks, fruit drinks, or juices as often as you drink water. You can stay refreshed, avoid headaches, keep your skin and hair healthy, and water doesn't have any sugars that can damage your teeth. The Food Standards Agency recommends drinking about 1.2 liters of fluids every day, which equals six to eight cups.

Foods that are raw, stir-fried, lightly microwaved, or cooked are the best ways to get the most vitamins from them. The more you boil vegetables, the more minerals and vitamins you lose. Plus, the stuff you end up with is sticky and gray. Ask your doctor to check your health first if you think you need a vitamin before you buy one.

Health Tip:

You don't need too much salt, sugar, caffeine and fizzy drinks.

Fun Ways to Stay Active

Endorphins and serotonin are "feel-good" chemicals released in your brain when you engage in physical activities like running or jogging.

When most people work out, they feel good because their bodies are doing what they're supposed to do: moving, pumping blood, and taking air in and out. Plus, what's not to love about dancing? This is indeed an exciting exercise!

Working out is important, but stretching is even more so. You can move freely and keep your muscles flexible. Tight and stressed muscles are more likely to get hurt. Stretching your muscles when they're warm is best, so do it after dancing or workout practice.

There are many good ways to stretch. Hold each pose for twenty seconds at a time, and don't bounce! Allow your body to sink into the pose. If a stretch hurts or feels squished, stop doing that pose. Talk to your doctor before starting any exercise or stretching routines if you are injured or have health issues.

It's important to keep in mind that if you're not fit or are heavier than you should be, you may get out of breath very quickly, or at least faster than someone who plays hockey nonstop every other night. Strangely, not working out can make you tired, which can make it harder to start. But once you do, you'll feel better.

- Do something, even if you don't think you can do it at the scheduled time.

- Start slowly, perhaps with a 10 or 15-minute stretching session.

- Begin with a daily 5-minute walk and gradually increase it to 30 minutes. Then, add 10 or 15 minutes each time until you reach an hour. It gets better. Do this hourly routine every day.

- Try walking for 30 minutes in the morning, 15 minutes at lunch, and 15 minutes to and from the bus stop. When you get home, take your dog for a walk around the block for a while.

- Take any chance to be active: walk to the store, get off the bus a stop or two early and walk the rest of the way, walk over to a friend's house to say hello instead of texting them, and take the longer route home.

- Remember that things you do every day are also activities: hanging out the laundry, vacuuming, going to work or school, dancing, messing around outside with friends, picking up trash, or delivering pamphlets.

- Choose something enjoyable to avoid boredom, or change your activities regularly.

- Set goals if that will help you get started. For example, you could join a team with regular practice and game times or decide to go for a quick walk four times a week. When you meet both big and small goals, you can keep track of them or treat yourself to flowers or a movie.

- Take a walk with some friends. It will be a good practice to take a walk with someone whose company you adore. It will keep you active and healthy. For example, you can talk while strolling through the park or while window shopping.

- If you want to speed up time, listen to music. But don't wear headphones when you're riding your bike on the road or crossing streets or paths. The music will distract you and block out other sounds.

Let's Laugh

I like to exercise because I really love to eat pizza.

Establishing Healthy Sleep Habits

Whether you are ready or not, school starts brutally early. So make sure you get enough rest. One study found a link between not getting enough sleep and getting worse grades. You know, having a good sleep makes you feel less sad. Sleep heals and strengthens your body's defenses. When it comes to life, sleep is the "chief nourisher in life's feast." Get more sleep if you've been feeling tired. Or, get up early at least once a week.

But if you sleep for half the day or take naps all the time, you might be using sleep as a way to escape. If you can't sleep, it might mean something is bothering you and you should talk about it. A lot of people don't mind falling asleep. If you do, don't drink coffee, cola, tea, or chocolate at night because they all have caffeine.

For people who are wide awake, a cup of milk or chamomile tea is a better choice. Don't work out too late at night, and know that watching a scary movie, yelling at your brother, or instant messaging a bunch of friends right before bed can wake you up instead of putting you to sleep.

It's better to take a bath and then read a book that's not for school. If you're still wide awake, avoid sleeping pills because they can be addictive. If you have trouble sleeping sometimes, try to see it as a chance to do something good, like studying, writing in a journal, or reading a short story.

When you're ready to sleep, put on something cozy and lie on your back on a hard mattress, preferably without a pillow or with one that is pretty flat. Not only is your spine straight, but none of your organs or limbs are squished. You also won't wake up with a crick in your neck or a cheek full of wrinkles from the sheets. Now, take slow, steady breaths through your nose from the bottom of your lungs. Picture yourself floating. One by one, tell your muscles to loosen up. Drift. Zzzzz.

Staying Clean: Hygiene Tips

Personal care is what you do for your body. As part of this habit, you should take a bath, wash your hands, brush your teeth, and do other things for personal hygiene regularly.

More than a million different germs and viruses touch you every day. They might stay on your body, and sometimes they might even make you sick. Taking care of your cleanliness may help you and the people around you stay healthy. They might also make you like the way you look.

Personal cleanliness helps you stay fresh, which can boost your confidence and make your relationships pleasant. It also lowers your risk of getting sick and other health problems that can come from not taking care of yourself properly.

The primary way we keep our bodies clean is through personal hygiene. Cleaning habits serve two primary purposes.

- To begin, being clean makes you safe. You may not be completely free of germs, but you are mostly free of the germs that are bad for you and could make you sick. Tooth decay, skin infections, and many other diseases that can be avoided can happen because of ignored personal hygiene.
- It helps you feel at ease when you're with other people. This could boost your confidence and self-esteem and encourage you to live a healthy life. When cleaning is part of who you are, it also helps you fit in with what society thinks of as mature behavior.

Keeping yourself clean is especially important during puberty when you experience new changes like growing body hair and changes in body odor. Hygiene helps you keep your private parts clean and stops body odor from happening.

Deodorants: If you have oily skin or hair, or you do exhausting tasks every day, you need to take a shower every day. If your skin is dry, you can take a bath on alternative days. Bathing too often removes the skin's natural oils that protect it. Different hair types need to be washed at other times, from once a day to once a week.

Whether to use deodorant or antiperspirant is a personal choice. You might want to get an antiperspirant if you have trouble sweating. When you use antiperspirants too much, they can block the sweat glands behind your arms. This can cause lumps that feel bad and may need to be checked out and treated by your doctor. It is always better to use deodorants and fragrant body wash instead of antiperspirants.

Dental Hygiene: Many diseases can be avoided by taking care of your teeth and gums. Some of the germs that can cause bad breath are killed when you brush your teeth. Getting rid of such bacteria also lowers the risk of getting several illnesses, such as cavities and gingivitis (an infection of the gums).

When you floss, you get rid of the germs and food that are stuck between your teeth. These bacteria might get into the bloodstream if they aren't killed. They could then cause heart disease, tooth loss, and gingivitis.

Nails: During puberty, you will like to let your nails grow out, shape them in different ways, and paint them. But toenails are an excellent place for bacteria to grow. If you eat with your hands, these germs could get into your mouth. If you touch your face, the germs could get into your mouth, eyes, and nose or stay on your skin. So, you need to keep your nails clean. You might use a nail brush to clean it up. Also, cutting your nails once a week should help get rid of dirt and debris and lower your risk of getting painful ingrown nails. Keep your nails short and neat by cutting them often.

Use a nail brush or a towel to clean off the buildup of dirt and germs under them. Keeping your nails clean keeps germs from getting into your mouth and other body holes. You should also not bite your nails.

Body Odor: When you get close to puberty, a new type of sweat gland starts to form and grows in your armpits and groin areas. Skin germs feed on the sweat produced by these glands, which can cause body odor.

Changing your clothes and washing your body often, especially after some hard exercise, can help keep germs from building up. It is essential to change your undergarments daily. Bacteria love to eat dead skin cells, sweat, and body fluids that get stuck in these clothes. That's why they smell bad.

Health Tips:

You might find these tips helpful if you want to improve your cleanliness and develop better habits:

- Remember to take a shower, wash your hair, cut your nails, or brush your teeth by setting an alarm on your phone. It will push you to do the thing, and after a while, you'll start to do it on your own.
- Put up a sign in the bathroom to remind you to wash your hands after using the bathroom. Remember to wash your hands before you eat by putting a small sign on the plates or bowls in the kitchen. These signs can help you remember things and improve your habits.
- It takes time to change a habit. Begin a new habit at the start of the week and give it your full attention. Do it every day for a week or two. When you're happy with it, add another one. You'll form the habits you want to have over time.

Why do Regular Health Checkups Matter?

Remember Ammy? Her story will tell you why regular health checkups are important.

After facing symptoms of hitting puberty, Ammy went to see her doctor the following week.

The doctor checked Ammy's body, measured her height, and did many tests during the visit. She then met up with Ammy and her mom to talk about the changes Ammy was going through. The doctor smiled and said, "Most girls hit puberty between the ages of eight and thirteen, but it can happen earlier or later. Some girls go through puberty so early or so quickly that they need special tests and medicine. Most girls, though, don't need any help. When you hit puberty, your body starts making hormones. Hormones are chemicals that tell your body what to do. That stuff in your body tells it to get bigger.

You and some other girls start going through puberty at age seven. Your body begins to grow and change in different ways during puberty. For instance, you might notice that your breasts are getting bigger. They might feel sore and painful as they grow."

In her mind, Ammy thought, "That's why the seat belt hurt across my chest." She felt relieved when she realized what was causing her discomfort.

The doctor continued speaking, and Ammy sat up straighter in her chair. What the doctor said helped her.

"You're taller now, and you might keep getting taller quickly. We call this a growth spurt. Three to four inches is an average amount of growth in a year! I think you should get longer pants right now so that you have room to grow. As your legs get longer, you can roll them up and then unroll them. Get shoes that are a little bigger than your feet. This way, your feet can grow, and you won't have to buy new shoes as often.

Ammy laughed and stretched her long legs out in front of her. She was thrilled about the thought of getting fresh clothes and shoes.

The doctor also said, "You may have also noticed that hair is growing under your arms." There may also be a strong smell in your armpits. We call this body odor. Body odor happens when germs in your sweat mix with the skin under your arms. This can make you smell bad. Showering or bathing every day is good for you. Use soap to clean your armpits while you're swimming. You can also get rid of smells by putting deodorant under your arms.

Ammy replied, "I have noticed hair under my arms, but not body odor yet."

She was feeling shy.

The doctor said, "Yes," and then asked, "Have you seen any pimples or oily skin on your face?" Ammy touched her face and said, "No, not really."

The doctor went on to say, "If you start to see bumps or pimples on your face or if you notice that it's getting oilier, wash your face gently once or twice a day with warm water and soap that doesn't have a scent." Also, use warm water to rinse the soap off. These steps will help keep your skin clean and may help you avoid getting acne (also written as pimples).

Your period is another vital part of puberty that will happen to you at some point. To explain, the doctor showed Ammy a picture.

"This is the first time a girl has her period. This means her body is getting bigger. This happens every month because an egg comes out of her ovary. It's not even close to an egg's size. As the egg gets ready to hatch, the uterus makes a lining that has some blood in it. She has a period flow every month, which means that her blood leaves her body through her vagina. You can get to your ovaries and vulva through the vagina.

For girls, however, breast growth is usually the first sign

of puberty. Each girl may have a different amount of time between when her breasts start to form and when her period starts. It can take years at times. It will be more fun to talk about this when that time comes around."

She put her head on her mom's arm. "Wow, that's a lot of changes!" she said. She smiled and said, "I do feel like I have a better grasp on what's going on with me and that these changes are normal." "Without a doubt," the doctor said. "At first, it can feel too much. Still, it helps a lot to know what to expect and that all of these changes are normal. Also, remember that these changes happen to everyone. Teenage years happen at different times for each person because it's up to their body."

Ammy's mom gave her a tight hug, which helped her feel better about understanding these changes.

"Along with changes in your body", the doctor said, "You may also notice changes in how you feel on the inside, in your thoughts and feelings. Some people may feel strange or self-conscious about their bodies as they grow and change."

Ammy remembered how she felt when she and Jada played dress-up.

She said with a slight frown, "I felt bad when my friend laughed at my body because it looked different from hers."

The doctor agreed and said, "Uh-huh—I can see why you're feeling embarrassed. You might want to let your friend know that these changes are because you are going through puberty. Keep telling her that she will go through puberty, too. Everyone does."

The doctor then asked, "Do your moods often change? You might feel joyful or thrilled one minute and then sad or angry the next."

The Ammy quickly leaned toward the doctor and exclaimed, "Yes, they do. Sometimes I'm happy and laughing, and then the next second, I'm sad and crying. Little things can bother me too. Is this okay?"

With a smile, the doctor made it clear, "Yes, that's just because your body is getting used to the changes. These mood swings will even out over time.

Ammy let out a sigh and pulled her mom closer. It made her feel so much better to know why she was having so many different emotions at once.

The doctor looked at Ammy and her mom. Her eyes were kind and warm.

"Coming up with different things to do when you're sad or having bad feelings can help. What are some things that might make you feel better at these times?"

"It helps to listen to music", Ammy said with a straight back. "Great!" "Any other ideas?" her mom asked. "Let's see," Ammy thought. "I could hang out with my dog, paint my nails, or read a book." The doctor agreed and said, "These are great ideas!"

Ammy's mom said, "Talking to someone you trust can also help you feel better. Like your mom? Or a good friend?" She asked Ammy.

"That's right!" agreed Ammy.

The doctor said, "Yes." "Ammy, one last thing to remember is that your body changes during puberty at its speed. You might feel a little weird going through changes before your friends, but they will also eventually go through puberty at some point."

"I understand now..." sighed Ammy with relief. Knowing what to expect and realizing that everyone goes through puberty was helpful to her.

That night at dinner, Ammy's mom talked about the trip to the doctor with Ammy's dad. "This morning, we went to see Dr. Dunn and learned about puberty and what it does to your body and mind." Ammy said, "There are a lot of changes."

Her dad gave her a warm smile. He said, "I'm glad you learned more about puberty." Dad also said, "Mom and I want you to know that we're always here for you if you need anything. We know quite a bit about puberty. Do you understand why?"

Ammy raised an eyebrow and gave it some thought. "Is it because you're older than 10?"

Laughing, her dad said, "Yes! We're here to help you as you change and grow." Mom said, "You can always talk to us," and then Ammy smiled and nodded in agreement.

As you read about Ammy's experience, you probably noticed how the doctor helped her understand puberty and the changes that come with it. The doctor also talked about ways to deal with these changes. That's why going for regular health checkups is important to keep your body healthy during these times.

A Note to Parents

It's not always easy to talk about cleanliness. Focus on talking about one thing at a time and keep it easy. Choose what you want to talk about, such as why it's important to use deodorant to control body odor.

Take a moment to think about how to bring up the subject in the most natural way. You could tell them, "Hey, I bought this for you at the store today," and show them the deodorant. As you grow older, around 16 years old, you might sweat more and have a stronger smell. Using deodorant can help you smell better. It's easy to use—just spray it under each arm, like this. Does that make sense?"

Part 7
Social Butterfly: Setting Your Circle

True friends are like diamonds—bright, beautiful, valuable, and always in style.

Nicole Richie

You can enjoy life more and have more fun if you have friends. It's time when you laugh so hard that your tummy hurts. You need to hang out together and share codes, words, and jokes that only your friends know. For example, you could write songs or plays together, take one another's stuff, go places together, be there for one another when things go wrong, and talk about anything.

It's about having a safe spot, but that spot is a person or a group of people.

Having friends is important for everyone. They make your life better. They make you happy and proud to be living. When you need extra care and attention, friends are very helpful.

You might feel like you don't have any people in your life who can help you or that you don't have many of them, and you're always alone. You might think that not having anyone to talk to and being alone makes you sad or depressed sometimes or most of the time.

If you live by yourself, this problem might get worse. Many people think that having at least five close friends and followers that they like in their lives would be helpful.

To keep your bonds strong, you need to take care of your relations regularly. How do you get in touch with people to make friends? It's not easy to do this. You might decide that staying at home is more comfortable for you than going to a place where you can meet new people. This is how almost everyone feels. It might help to ignore those feelings and go to neighborhood events where you might meet new people with whom you could become closer friends. Friendships are an important part of our social lives, and they can have a direct effect on your mood and how you feel.

Making New Friends

Being honest attracts honesty. When you're true to yourself, you'll naturally connect with people who share your interests. And sometimes you "click" with someone without really understanding why. Of course, you can't always tell when you meet someone for the first time if they'll be a good match and you are likely to become good friends.

Don't just wait to be chosen. If you want to find a good friend, be patient instead of letting someone who is too bossy, boring, or mean choose you as their friend. Also, don't pretend to be someone you're not just to make someone like you; it's too hard to keep up with.

There are times when the person you choose doesn't want to be your friend. It might be hard, but you need to move on. Still, it's a lot better than sitting there like a box of cereal, waiting for someone, anyone, to pick you up. Not everyone needs to be your friend or like you. Just a few sincere friends are enough.

Who are the right friends for you?

True friends: Friends who like each other and have similar interests can be together as true friends. Sharing the same interests, keeping each other's secrets, making time for each other (not just when it's convenient for them), listening to each other and trying to understand how the other person feels can make lasting bonds of friendships.

True friends are loyal, stand up for each other, and never join in when someone else is being mean. You should not mind if your friends have different ideas, clothes, or hobbies.

It can be hard to make new friends if you're shy. And who isn't shy and takes a while to get used to new people? It might seem like school is the best place to make friends, but there are plenty of other places where you can meet people too.

To turn strangers into good friends, you need to spend time getting to know them. When you meet someone for the first time, don't tell them your deepest, darkest secrets or ask them very personal questions. This could turn them off. You should feel like you belong without needing to be exactly like everyone else. Make friends with people who appreciate you and value your differences. Don't be a part of a circle where you don't feel accepted, comfortable, or valued.

Having some good friends means you can be proud of yourself. You can have space and time for yourself. And nobody objects to the way you dress and look. Nobody is the boss in your group of friends and everyone gets along easily. There is no bad name-calling and no making fun of each other.

Let's Laugh

There's nothing better than a friend, unless it's a friend with a lot of gifts.

How to Communicate Effectively

The most important part about having a buddy is making sure you can talk to them without worrying about what they think.

Here are a few suggestions for you:

1. Listening is very important in friendships. A lot of people like to talk but they don't really listen to what the other person is saying. When you pay attention to what your friend is saying, you will eventually build a strong bond of friendship. Your friend will listen to you attentively in return.

2. You can practice some good communication skills if you talk to your friends outside school or in your busy schedule. Use lunch breaks as a way to talk to them. Or maybe talk to them over the weekend and enjoy a party together.

3. Everyone needs their own space, so don't feel guilty about it. It's important to have boundaries, like knocking on your door before anyone enters your room. Select your hobbies; watch your favorite TV shows, listen to your favorite music, and show up to your sports practices. Keep being interested in what you are doing.

4. You often have trouble with your friends' changing sense of who you are and need to feel loved. Talk to yourself a lot. Show your love by appreciating yourself in any way that makes you feel good.

5. Honor your achievements, let yourself know you understand when you make a mistake, listen to yourself when you need help, and be interested in how you intend to resolve the issue. Help yourself figure out how to solve your problems.

6. Every young person needs to feel included and special to have a healthy sense of self-esteem in communication. Take time to relax and enjoy yourself. Positive thoughts can bring people together.

Understanding Crushes and Relationships

There will likely be many relationships in your life. Girls today often wait longer to get married, have kids, or move out of their parents' house. You'll experience breaking someone's heart, having your heart broken, thinking you've found 'The One', being wrong, getting over it, making mistakes, and then falling in love again.

There may be a racing heartbeat, sweaty palms, flushed cheeks, tingly bits, nausea, dilated pupils, loss of appetite, extreme happiness and crushing disappointment, complete self-consciousness, being curious to know exactly where the other person is even if you're trying not to notice, not being able to think about much else, and not being able to focus. Of course, these signs can also be used for a short-term crush, a short-term attraction, and some tropical conditions.

When you have a crush on someone, you like them but don't always do anything about it. You just look at them with admiration and blush whenever they come close, and then you get a crush on someone else. A lot of girls have at least one crush on a stranger. A crush is usually on a famous person, like an actor, singer, or athlete.

When you're in a healthy relationship, you:

- Trust and respect each other.
- Are honest with each other.
- Can be "yourself" and not have to put on a show.
- Keep talking and listening to each other.
- Disagree or argue without fighting all the time.
- Both can say sorry.
- Don't have to spend all your time together.
- Agree on some things, but not all of them; agree that each partner would "call it off" before starting something with someone else or telling other people you're available; and don't care if the other person doesn't smile or wears ugly shoes.

Relationship Tip:
Give up now if the other person isn't interested in being with you. Anything else will be a waste of time.

Everyone, even rich and popular people, breaks up with someone. That's why there are so many songs about broken hearts. And every sad song seems to be about you while you're going through it. If you think it's making you sad and your family and friends can't help, see a counselor. Your doctor can help you find one.

If you're feeling down, listen to music, watch movies that touch your heart, and talk to your friends about your feelings. When you're ready, switch to songs and movies that cheer you up, remind yourself that you're strong, and believe in yourself. It takes time to heal a broken heart, but you'll feel better.

Dealing with Peer Pressure

A peer group is a group of people who are around the same age and have similar backgrounds, interests, and likes or dislikes, such as a school's theater group. (It can also mean all people of the same age and level of experience, like kids.) Being in a group can sometimes mean that everyone starts doing the same things, whether they are aware of it or not. (Having the same styles and doing the same things like piercings, blonde with a fake tan, or something else).

You feel like you have to be like them when you're with bad friends. You'll get frozen out if you don't say and do the 'right' things. Picture yourself hanging out with the cool kids. It might not be as fun as it seems. It might even be like being a doll in hell.

Peer pressure is when you feel like you have to change how you act, look, what you like, or what you say to please your friends or be accepted by them. This is an example of peer pressure: Someone tells you what to wear and you know that people will make fun of you or be mean if you don't wear what everyone else is wearing.

You copy other people to feel like you're more likeable and doing the right thing because you don't trust yourself. You might lose your sense of reason when you're under a lot of pressure from your friends. Remember how much more trouble you could get into as a child if you were with a friend, brother, sister, or neighbor than if you were by yourself? It can feel like you have to do something when you're with your siblings, like putting mashed banana on the couch pillows, 'borrowing' your mom's lipstick, or giving the dog beer. There are times when it can happen to you as a child, teen, or adult. It may be true that 'it seemed like a good idea at the time,' but that doesn't make it the smartest idea ever.

People will try to get you to do or say something you don't want to. Learn to say "No."

You might be thinking why it's good to be pushed by your friends. Yes, kids do tell each other to do dangerous things, but that's not all that peer pressure is. Group pressure can also be good for you in many ways.

Your friends may teach you some good things and tell you to do what they say.

Like if you see your friends doing something good for a cause, you might want to do the same thing. This will help you make changes for the better. Following your friends' good habits might make your life and thoughts better (change for the better). If you pick out some good habits from your friends, group pressure can be good for you.

Being exposed to peer pressure will give you a great chance to learn about what other people like and think because people behave in very different ways. This will give you a chance to pick the best from what most people have to offer. Your peers may give you ideas or push you to make a positive change in your life. Because of this, group pressure might also work in your favor and help you make the right choices.

Setting and Respecting Personal Boundaries

As you get older, it's important to learn how to set limits, both in your physical and mental world. Having respectful, helpful, and healthy friendships and dating partnerships are also very important.

Well, this is really strange that a lot of girls fail to set suitable limits with their friends or the person they are dating. This makes them more likely to be bullied or abused in a relationship.

Making rules isn't always easy, though. You have to stand up for yourself and draw lines in the sand because it's rough. Also, letting other people know your boundaries can lead to tough talks or awkward situations. There are more kinds of boundaries than just physical ones. If someone is saying things that make you feel bad about how you look, it's okay to let them know how you feel. The unfollowing of social media accounts that make you feel bad about your body or that focus too much on changing your looks is another help code. *Does it matter what someone from the internet says about what you should do with your body?* No! Try to get good follows.

The most important thing to do to fix body image problems is to stop having a bad view of yourself. Remember that the way your body looks naturally is how it looks. Instead of watching the news about Photoshop, get rid of all the beliefs that are stopping you from enjoying what makes you unique!

If you can't think of anything fun to do on campus, look at the events schedule to see what outside or on-campus activities are happening. For girls who love going to the gym, there are also gyms close and on campus that students can use.

Setting healthy limits for yourself will keep you safe physically and mentally without trying to control yourself. You will find out what you want and need without hurting someone else's rights or needs.

To give you some examples for setting boundaries:

- Telling someone that you want to take things slowly in a love relationship and making sure that you are not pressured to do more than you want to.

- You can ask someone to stop making fun of you about a sensitive topic and give them a punishment if they do, like spending less time with them.

- Tell a friend that you don't feel good about drinking and ask them to support your decision not to drink.

- Friends who borrow money a lot and don't pay it back should be told that they won't be able to borrow money from you again until they pay back what they owe.

- You can let a brother know that you need time to yourself and ask him to respect this need by not entering your room when the door is closed.

- You can ask your love partner to respect your time with other people by not calling or texting you a lot while you're with other people.

Knowing when to set rules and when to be flexible is important. It helps you understand what's okay and what's not, so you can feel comfortable and safe.

To give you some examples:

- Keeping everyone out of your life and not trusting anyone.

- You want your friends or potential dates to be there for you whenever you need them.

- Thinking that other people know what you are feeling or thinking and should react in the same way.

- Saying yes to friends or dates even if it goes against what you think.
  Going against what you believe or what you stand for to fit in, be liked, or make other people happy.

A Note to Parents

As you talk to your child about growing up and puberty, show them that you are ready and willing to talk. Make sure they know they can always talk to you about anything. Don't be too pushy or clear. There's no need to rush or talk about all of this right now.

You should take the chance to talk whenever they give it to you. Life does get busy, but most of the time, they only need five or ten minutes of your time. Try to get them to talk about how they feel about change and growing up. Talk to them about what they're excited about and what worries them. Make it normal.

Part 8
Your Digital World: E-Learning

Your online reputation is your reputation. Protect it.

Tyler Tervooren

How can you learn to use the internet, email, chat rooms, and blogs safely? Cell phones, social media, messaging, and blogs can sometimes be used by mean people to spread lies. They're also places where some creeps might look for people to bother.

Tips for safety

Here are some safety tips to remember when you're on the computer.

- Don't let anyone take a picture or video of you that you wouldn't want your parents to see online, like when you're drunk or without a shirt on. Pictures taken with cell phones and webcams can be put on the Internet and seen by a huge number of people.

- Be very careful about what you write and post on a blog, in an online group, or on a social networking site. It's important to remember that things you post online can be seen by your parents, teachers, bosses, and anyone else you know. They might even share or repost it.

- Do not let anyone see what you do on the social sites you use. This is called "privacy settings." These settings let you decide who can see what you post on your pages and keep strangers from seeing your private notes, photos, and information.

- Remember that your account is only as safe as you make it. If you friend every Tom, Dick, and Harry you meet online, your information will not be kept secret.

- Send emails that you wouldn't want to be shared all over the world. One girl sent a guy a sexy message, and the next thing she knew, he had sent it to a friend, who then sent it to more friends, and so on. It had reached over 100,000 people, including her parents, teachers, and newspapers and blogs in other countries, with her name still on it.

- It's not okay for people to send you inappropriate pictures or information through email or cell phone, or to share it where you work or study. It's not allowed. Tell your service provider or the person in charge of the site if you get a sexual or creepy message.

- If unnecessary sites keep showing up on your computer at work, school, or home, tell a parent, teacher, or boss. They might be able to change the 'security settings' on the computer to stop the sites from showing up. If you tell a teacher or boss, they won't think you went to the sites on purpose, which could lead to suspension or firing.

Let's Laugh

Social media is a stage for actors who are overreacting.

Staying Safe on Social Media

The internet is great! We use it to stay in touch with family and friends, study for school projects, learn more about our hobbies and interests, and have fun. Some people who use the internet and some things that can happen on it can be dangerous, so it's important to do what you can to stay safe.

It's important to know that nothing is private on the Internet or when you text or talk on the phone. You should never write something online or send it through email or text message that you don't want everyone to see. These people may include your best friend, worst enemy, teacher, director, mom, grandma, and so on. It's simple to send private pictures, documents, or videos because of how simply email works. But once the pictures or information are out there, it's almost impossible to get them back!

An electronic way to talk to someone is like a big sign on a highway close to your home. Don't send messages or emails with things you wouldn't want everyone to see on a big poster.

Also, keep in mind that almost everyone on the Internet is a stranger. You know your parents told you not to talk to strangers, right? If a stranger contacts you in a chatroom or email, you should tell your parents or another adult. This is true even if they say they are a kid. Also, never, ever, ever agree to meet up with someone you met online without first getting permission from your parents. This could be a really dangerous trap!

Lastly, remember that many bad things can happen online when you're a pre-teen or teenager. Friends vote on each other's looks in 'Beauty Pageants,' and kids feel like outsiders because of cyberbullying. It's easy to get caught up in the bad side of social networking. You can change this, though. Be a good person in your online group. Do not take part in insulting games or add to a rant that will hurt someone's feelings. Instead, fill your cyberspace with love, respect, and peace.

Practicing Good Digital Manners

Nowadays, everyone spends a lot of time working online through social networking sites, emailing, texting, chat rooms, and just surfing the web.

Because of this, you should go over these cyber etiquette tips.

1. **Follow the Golden Rule.** Treat others the way you want them to treat you. Don't talk to someone online in a way you wouldn't talk to them in person.

2. **Keep in mind that anyone can see everything you post online.** It doesn't matter if you delete the text or letter. It can be found if you've released it. You leave a digital footprint when you post something online.

3. **DON'T use ALL CAPS.** when you email or post something. If you use ALL CAPS, in the internet language, it shows that you are yelling!

4. **Stay kind in your talk.** Even if you don't see the other person on the screen, stay kind. It shouldn't make you rude as the person sitting on the other side of the screen is a human just like you.

5. **Avoid posting when you are angry.** You should not post something after being mad. Take some time to calm down before you do anything about it. It might be possible that when angry you write or post something which you later regret.

6. **Use unique login and passwords.** If you use the same login and password on different websites and applications, then there are chances that you can easily get hacked. Use different

passwords and create different logins. The hackers might get an idea of who you are and what you do if they get access to any of your accounts. Use nicknames, and combinations of alphabets, numbers and symbols to create passwords.

7. **Come up with good email names.** People will use your email address to get in touch with you when you apply to schools, jobs, or awards. Make sure your email address is correct and is not embarrassing or childish.

8. **Don't post pictures you don't want others to see.** Don't post your personal pictures on social media if you don't want many people to see them. If it's a picture of a friend, ask yourself if their parents would want that picture to be shared or seek your friends' permission. Let people know the meaning of 'no' by not publishing it.

9. **Don't talk to people you don't know.** Don't open up about private things about yourself in chat rooms. Cyber friends can be fake, even if you feel like you know the person you're chatting with online.

10. **Don't email or post private information about yourself.** Do not share your passwords, social security numbers, home addresses, phone numbers, passwords, family names, or credit card numbers with anyone, and never your full name.

Balancing Screen Time and Real Life

These days, screens are both an important and a controversial part of everyone's lives. Be careful about how much time you spend in front of screens. It can affect your body and your mind.

Kids who spend too much time in front of a screen are more likely to have mental and physical health problems. This means you should limit your screen time not just for your eyes, but for your overall health.

An open conversation with your family about screen time is a good place to start. Studies have shown that having limits for screen time and activity has positive effects.

There are three easy rules you can talk to yourself that will help keep your eyes healthy and lower your risk of eye infections.

The elbow rule. This is where you should try to keep the space between your eyes and anything close to them between your arm and wrist. When you read, any screen or book should be no closer than where your elbow is. Make a fist and put it next to your eyes. This helps you stay away from watching distances of less than 20 to 30 cm, which can make it harder to see, cause myopia (when you can see things up close but things far away look blurry), and make it hard for your eye muscles to work properly.

The 20/20 rule. When you read or work on a screen, you should take a 20-second break after every 20 minutes. You should look across the room for 20 seconds to calm down the muscles in your eyes that help you focus before starting to read or use a computer again. To keep your eyes healthy, don't look at things up close for too long. Staring at something for more than 45 minutes straight has been linked to myopia.

The two-hour rule. This means that after school, you should only use screens for fun or relaxation for up to two hours a day.

How to Evaluate Online Information

Kids should have many chances to learn how important it is to question the information they find online and offline. Your curriculum can be a great way to get to see things from different points of view and think about things in new ways. Adults like structured and clear-cut thinking prompts that aren't just a list of things to do. They also like prompts that ask for evidence to back their thinking. Teens also like to work on these problems in small groups and then get together with the family to share their ideas.

I'll give you a list of strategies that you can use to improve your online research skills.

- Is this site useful for what I want to do?
- What is this site meant to do?
- Who put the information on this site together, and how knowledgeable is that person?
- When was the last time this site's information was changed?
- Where can I go to make sure this information is correct?
- What made this person or group post this on the internet?
- Does the website only show one side of the problem, or does it show more than one?
- What does the author's point of view mean for the information and pictures on this site?
- Could the information on this site hurt or offend anyone?
- What do these ideas have to do with my questions and thoughts?

Protecting Your Privacy Online

Here are some tips on how to keep your privacy online:

- In an email, chat room, or blog, never put your real last name, your address, your phone number, or your neighborhood or town. Phone number, street location, school sports team name, or anything else can help others figure out where you are.

- Be careful not to give away too much information in what you write or show, like a picture of a nearby location, your house, or the name of the nearby shopping. Just say 'London' or 'the Scottish Highlands' as your place of residence. That way, really weird people won't be able to find you.

- If you want to get something 'free' or look at something on a website, don't give them your email address or any other information. This is often a trick to get your information so that someone can find you and either send you annoying ads or try to get your banking information to steal from you.

- You should be careful about what information you give out online. If you are under 18, you should always ask a parent first. In case you have a bank account, never share your bank or other financial information over the Internet, even if someone emails you and asks for it.

- Do not meet someone you met online by yourself. Girls go to these kinds of meetings all over the world every year and then disappear. Many others have been harassed by men who set up the meeting by pretending to be a girl, a young man, or someone nice. These people would try to be extra nice to trap you. It would feel like you can trust this person and there's no harm in having a face-to-face talk but that's really really risky.

- If you want to meet someone you met online, you should inform a parent and friends know where you're going. Meet at your house while a parent who knows about it is at home; or meet in a public place with lots of other people, like a shopping mall or cafe, with a parent, an adult friend, or more than one friend of your age.

- Attachments in emails from people you don't know should not be opened or replied to.

- Do not send money, a bank account number, or a reply to someone who emails and says they will send you money, lottery winnings, or a fortune (money left to you in a will). Even if the email looks professional, it could still be a scam.

Also, never talk to someone on the phone about your
- banking details. It's a good way for thieves to steal money. Scammers can send out thousands of spam emails and calls, and only one person out of every 100 might answer and be scammed.

A Note to Parents

You should make a rule about how long your kid can be on the computer. There is nothing a machine can ever do that a human can. Keep your children's lives from being completely dominated by the internet; too much of anything can be harmful.

You have to assist your child in maintaining a healthy balance between computer use and face-to-face communication. Technology may be exciting and always evolving, but one thing never changes: people still need to be able to communicate with one another. Instruct your child on the appropriate use of technology.

Part 9
A Better You: Self-Perception

The most powerful relationship you will ever have is the relationship with yourself.

Steve Maraboli

Connect with yourself and work on yourself daily. There are going to be a lot of people in your life who might put you down. You should stay away from such people. Do the things that make you happy and productive.

In what ways are you special?
How do you maintain good relations?
What sets you apart?
What do you like the most about yourself?

Keep exploring your uniqueness. Discover yourself: your likes, dislikes, interests, and hobbies. It can be nice to look and act like everyone else. But it's better to be yourself and not be like everyone else. Learn more about yourself. Pay attention to your dreams at night and during the day. You can blend in with the current trends when you want to, but be proud of what makes you unique.

Learning to Love Yourself

A lot of people all over the world are obsessed with their bodies' small flaws. When we have a bad opinion of our bodies, we often avoid certain events and activities, like going to the beach, because we're afraid of being seen in a swimming suit that shows a lot.

Being unhappy with the way we look can also cause problems in relationships.

When we lose confidence, we might stick to what we know and what makes us feel safe instead of going after the things we want to do. People who get stuck in negative thoughts might get up and start an immediate practice such as exercise or dieting but these efforts probably won't have any long-term benefits.

You want to find a way to take care of yourself, right? That's great! People often forget to take care of themselves, but it's important for their overall health. If you want to live a long and happy life, take care of your body, mind, and heart.

When you make up your mind about something that this thing is not going to work, it definitely won't. Your mind is like a magnet, it attracts both positive and negative energy. That's why you feel irritated after meeting someone grumpy.

Start accepting your body. Don't let the society tell you what a perfect body looks like. You should be healthy, that's all that matters. Check your Body Mass Index (BMI) and see if you need to work on your body.

Once you start to think more positively and love your body, the pieces will start to fit together. I have already said that it is very important to give your body the nutrients it needs and to stop eating foods that are bad for you. The idea of diets and losing weight needs to go away, and you need to focus on how food affects your body.

Nothing should be more satisfying than doing something that feeds your soul, like watching Netflix, reading a book, or even just going around the neighborhood and taking in the sights. Sometimes watching TV more than your scheduled time is fine, but if you do it all the time, it won't be good for your mind and eyes. Watch something on Netflix that makes you think, inspires you, or broadens your mind.

Pick up a book that feeds your soul and brings joy and life to you. Read some comic books if you want to have some funny read. Anything that teaches you something positive will motivate you and keep your mind active. It will also make you want to make a change, even if it's just in your own life.

Look at the sky. You should travel more if you haven't already, even if you stay in your own country. Just go somewhere you've never been before and look around. I feel better and more alive every time I see something new. You will never regret going to a new place, and it will make you feel great. So, get out there and enjoy some great things and beautiful places. Trust me, those moments will make you so happy for a long time.

Let's Laugh

I could be as famous as Harry Potter but I misplaced my wand.

Making Healthy Choices

A person's puberty years may be both the best and worst of their lives. During this time in your life, you might find it hard to make choices that keep you safe and healthy because you'll face tough situations.

Girls use the puberty period to shape their identities and gain independence in their communities! These are the years to make major decisions regarding your family, education, and social life. You may not always succeed when you take chances, whether it's by trying out for the school play, joining a new table at lunch, or making a challenging play on the football field.

However, you are more likely to become more aware of your capabilities and recognize areas in which you can advance. As you experiment with freedom, you may find it beneficial to take calculated risks with peers. Your brain's reward centers get excited about these challenges! That's why children are naturally curious and eager to explore new things and discover what the world has to offer.

You always have choices to make. Some decisions are made quickly and based on intuition. Many girls don't often think about decisions that could affect their whole life, like what to wear, what to eat for lunch, or which way to go to work. These girls frequently feel confused during the decision-making process.

However, we often fear not knowing what will happen after making decisions more than the decisions themselves. People aren't scared of being up high; they're scared of falling. Effective and smart decision-making is a skill that is acquired throughout life experience. While you may not always be conscious of it, making judgments is a skill we acquire throughout infancy.

Depending on how much fun you have with a particular toy, you will nearly always choose to play with it. Although this conclusion may seem simple and intuitive, there is still a process involved in making decisions.

Practical decision-making abilities can help you manage your stress levels better.

Every day, you make decisions that could change your life. However, the majority of girls never receive instruction on how to make sound decisions. Consequently, many girls find it difficult if they are given choices such as:

- Should I get good math scores or work on geography?
- How should I respond when my friend offers to buy me a drink?
- Should I approach someone to go on a date?

Decisions made during puberty can indeed have long-term consequences that extend beyond high school. Adolescents often encounter challenges such as transitioning to high school, choosing subjects, navigating bullying, forming friendships, and handling test anxiety, all of which require making important choices.

Learning to make good choices is important. So, it's a good idea to practice by picking an after-school activity you like or talking about a new bedtime with your family.

These five strategies will assist you in making wise decisions for your education and personal life.

1. Determine the choice: You can make better selections if you are clear about the goal you have in mind and the problem you want to solve. Take on a problem when you're composed and apply reason rather than just feeling. This way you can come up with good solutions. Don't make any choices that can affect you or your family in negative ways.

Trust your gut feeling because there will be times when you feel strong emotions and feelings about a decision. Understand the point of view of your parents as well to see if they are saying the same thing as your heart and mind. See all the pros and cons of a choice or situation and future-forward your brain and see if it works well for you. You can ask yourself the following questions:

- Is this something I want?

- How did I end up thinking about it?

- How can I benefit from it in the long run?

2. Brainstorm about it: You can ask yourself these questions:

- What is the issue I am attempting to solve?

- What do I want to achieve?

- What is the best outcome I'm aiming for?

3. Think over it: See if the choices you have in your mind can benefit you. Ask yourself these questions:

- Will it help me reach my goal?
- Is it telling the truth?
- Is it fair and safe for everyone involved?

When you make a choice, you have to follow it. Are you ready to take on so many duties? Know what your choice could mean before you make it. This will help you learn from it and take responsibility for it.

4. Make the choice: Once you have made up your mind about your choice and want to make it happen, do let your parents know about it. As they might help you in making it happen.

5. Revisit your choice: Think about your choice and see how it turned out to be for everyone. Find a good time to think about what you learned while making your decision. You might ask yourself these things:

- What did I find out about myself?
- What's important to me?
- What should I do the same next time I have to decide?

Remember to say positive things to yourself. It's not easy to make decisions, and you may find it even harder with all the changes and stresses you're facing. When you praise what you have done and how you have taken responsibility, it will give you strength and make you want to try again.

Expressing Your Unique Style

Different groups of people can have very different ideas about what fashion means at any given time.

Every style has one thing in common: it changes all the time. Styles are a great way to see how fashion has changed over time, what looks good now, and how clothing can be an art form.

The reason fashion always changes could be because it's fun! Businesses make more money when people think they need new clothes all the time, even after they've fit better. Adults with their own money often run fashion pages and TV shows. They also get so much free stuff from makeup and fashion companies as 'samples' (or bribes) that it's easy for them to change what they wear all the time.

Fashion writers make advertisers happy by showing off new clothes and looks and saying that some things are 'essential' when they're just extras that you can choose not to have. People who work in fashion don't pay attention for long.

Style and fashion are not the same thing, though 'in style' can mean 'in fashion.' Fashion changes all the time and is mostly for people who care what other people think and don't want to stand out more than everyone else.

Style is more personal; it's a look that fits your attitude, creativity, and body type. It's "you" and what you like, not what's in stores. I think most of us try on a lot of different styles in our teens and twenties until we find one or a few styles that we like, that express our uniqueness, and that are easy to carry. A signature style is a way of dressing that always fits with a certain theme that a lot of people find and stick with.

You don't arrive with style already present. You have to try a lot of different things and fail a lot before you find your style.

Here are some ideas:

- When you're hungry and dizzy or tired but need to 'get something,' don't go shopping for clothes. It's not a good idea to buy cheap clothes just to entertain yourself.

- Put on clothes that fit you.

- Don't stress too much about what other people might or might not like. You'll look great if you're sure of yourself.

- Check to see if your 'good' clothes are good for you. You will feel and look uncomfortable and 'wrong' if you wear a skirt that is so short that you have to pull it down all the time and can't bend over.

- Consider visiting a thrift store, exploring a new type of store, or going shopping with an adult whose style you admire.

Planning for Your Future

As humans, we need to set goals for what we want to achieve and work towards them. Getting to your goals might not always be easy but having goals, no matter how big or small, is part of what makes life worth living. Overall, it makes you happy because it gives you a sense of what's important, helps you figure out where you want to go, and keeps you interested and active.

As for most people, they have a clear idea of what or who they want to be in the future. At the very least, everyone has values and hobbies that shape what they want from life. Still, it might be hard to come up with acceptable goals that you'll work toward for some years.

It might be overwhelming to know where to start, and your goals might seem impossible to reach. But if you're ready, you might be able to set goals for your life that are just as fun to work toward as they are to reach.

Most of the time, people mix up aims with resolutions or goals. Like goals, objectives can be set for any part of life, such as health, money, school, and so on. A lot of people only have a vague idea of what they want out of life. In this first step, your goal is to start putting ideas like "happiness" or "security" into things you want to do.

Take out a pen and paper and begin writing down the things that are important to you. At this point, it's fine to be general, but try not to be vague. Let's say the first thing that comes to mind is "happy." That's fine. But try to explain what that idea means. What does the word "happy" mean to you? What does a happy life look like to you?

The key to your success is reminding yourself that you are where you are because of your choices. Right now, you're in this place because you decided to be here. There's no better time than now to start turning your dreams into reality.

Spreading Kindness and Positivity

BE Kind

You will probably have days when you worry about how you look every so often. Your mind might be focused on a zit or the way your hair doesn't look quite right. It sounds like you might be feeling self-conscious because your braces feel tighter now.

That dull pain after getting my braces tightened was always my least favorite part. (I thought about them more than usual.) No matter what is making you think about how you look, keep in mind that you are more focused on the bad things than anyone else. Put on a smile and think about something good instead of having small things ruin your day. People will only see your bright, happy smile and not the little things that are making you sad. Also, a smile will make you feel better!

Studies have shown that your brain reads your facial emotions. Really! So the next time you want to look and feel sure of yourself, think about something that makes you happy. Your brain would do the same.

Be yourself. Accept, love, and love who you are. It's your unique attitude that makes you who you are.

Be humble. Do not let your pride get in the way. This will make you feel bad, which is not good or healthy. Do not indulge in a superiority complex and believe that you are better than any other person on Earth. It will cause arrogance to grow in you which is not a good trait.

Be nonjudgmental. You don't need to check yourself against someone else. You don't need to find things that make you and someone else's personalities different. We are all different. You have a personality that makes you different from other people, and that's fine.

A Note to Parents

Most of the time, if your child is big enough to ask, they're ready to hear the answer. In other words, being open and honest is the best way to answer their questions.

When they ask a question, you should answer it as if it were any other question they get every day. That way, they won't think the subject is embarrassing. No matter how old your child is, keep your answers brief, factual, and positive. Most of the time, they will ask for more details if they need it. You might even ask them if that answers their question or if they still need more help.

Conclusion:
Stay Active and Positive

You already know that your body goes through a lot of changes during puberty. The fact that you are growing up and becoming an adult might make you feel very "up," proud, and happy. During puberty, most of you also have some not-so-great thoughts every once in a while. As a preteen, you all get the "blues," which are times when you feel sad or down, sometimes for no clear reason. The chemicals your body is making may play a role in why you feel this way.

There will be times when you feel like you can't control your body when you go through puberty. It could be stressful because you don't know what would happen next or how everything would end. How much taller are you going to get? What size will your breasts grow to be? When will you have your first periods? These questions bring both happiness and sadness, and times make you confused. It's normal to feel this way — it can be a lot to take in.

Growing up brings about changes, but it doesn't change who you are. In the end, you're still the same person, but with new skills and situations that make you a better person.

Remember that you are still you when you feel like you can't handle things. Also, you're great!

Appendices

Glossary of Helpful Terms

- **Acne:** Skin condition with pimples or spots that can appear during puberty.
- **Bra:** An undergarment which is worn to support the breasts.
- **Cramps:** Pain in the belly which some girls feel during their periods.
- **Discharge:** A fluid that releases from the vagina before the periods begin.
- **Epilator:** A tool that is used to remove hair from the roots.
- **Fatigue:** The feeling of tiredness which can sometimes happen during puberty.
- **Growth spurt:** A period of rapid growth during puberty.
- **Hygiene:** A practice of staying clean to feel good and healthy.
- **Identity:** Your understanding of yourself.
- **Journaling:** The process of writing your thoughts to understand them better.
- **Kindness:** Staying nice to yourself and others during tough times.
- **Leg hair:** The hair that grows on legs during puberty years.
- **Menstrual cup:** A silicone cup that goes into the vagina to catch period blood.
- **Nutrition:** The healthy food you eat to stay fit.
- **Ovaries:** Two small organs in the female body that produce eggs.
- **Pad:** A one-time use or reuse item with layers that absorb menstrual blood.
- **Quiet time:** Time to relax to become calm and composed.

- **Razor:** A tool which is used to cut the hair from the surface of the skin.
- **Superstitions:** An idea that isn't based on facts but is accepted by a lot of people.
- **Taboo:** Something which is not openly talked about.
- **Uterus:** An organ in the body of girls where babies are formed.
- **Vagina:** The opening in the female body connecting the outer genitals with the uterus.
- **Well-being:** The state of being happy and fit.
- **X-chromosome:** The type of chromosome that determines the gender of a person.
- **Yeast infection:** A common infection of the vagina that can cause itching and discharge.
- **Zits:** Small bumpy spots like pimples on the skin.

Positive Affirmations

Make an affirmation gem box to use the power of affirmations for good. Put decorated gems or stones in a small box. Put different statements on each gem and put them in the box. Affirmations like "I deserve love, happiness, and success" can be written down. Some examples can be:

- I embrace my uniqueness and celebrate my individuality.
- I am confident in my abilities and trust my judgments.
- I believe that I can achieve anything I set my mind to.
- I am determined and can overcome any challenge that comes my way.

Any gem will do. Hold it while saying the statement when you need a boost. Keep it with you all day to help you remember. Accept the good energy and let the affirmations help you get stronger and move forward.

Recommended Books and Websites

Name of website: Preteen Health Talk

Where is it? http://www.pamf.org/preteen/

Who runs it? The Palo Alto Medical Foundation

Find tons of information about your changing body. Also includes sections on your feelings, growing up, and sharing. Make sure to check out the interactive section on bullying.

Name of website: Young Women's Health

Where is it? www.youngwomenshealth.org

Who runs it? Center for Young Women's Health / Children's Hospital of Boston

A very extensive website with all sorts of information about young women's health. The information is divided into larger categories like nutrition and fitness, emotional health, and development. Some of the information is unique, like tips on creating a healthy vegetarian diet for a pre-teen girl.

Name of website: Teen in Charge: Teen Health

Where is it? http://www.teensincharge.org/

Who runs it? The Chinese Community Health Resource Center

This site has lots of helpful health information, including details about your body, and your emotions, and videos on how to make healthy choices.

Book 1:

- My Body, My Self Book for Girls By Lynda Madaras

Book 2:

- What's Happening to My Body By Lynda Madaras

FAQs: Common Questions Answered

1. Does every girl go through puberty?

Yes, but each girl will have a unique experience that is both the same and different from other girls. Some girls hit puberty earlier than others, but most girls go through the basic things: getting bigger, getting breasts, getting acne and body odor, unexpected hair growth, and having periods. You won't believe it, but even boys go through puberty.

2. When is everything going to happen for me?

Height and weight gain are common signs of puberty in girls. However, many girls don't realize they are going through it because they have been growing their whole lives! When girls first notice they are going through puberty, they often notice when their breasts start to grow. For girls, this is the first change in their bodies that comes with puberty. Teenage years usually begin for girls between the ages of eight and eleven. Teenage years can start up to two years earlier for girls than for boys!

3. Can puberty make you lazy?

What you do to take care of your body can change how you grow during puberty. There is so much going on. Your bodies need healthy food and enough sleep to stay strong. Your brain and bloodstream contain chemicals that help you grow. These chemicals work while you sleep because your brain and body need to make growth happen.

4. In your puberty years, what kind of food is best to eat?

During puberty, girls need to make sure they get enough calcium in their foods. Your body uses calcium better as a teen than as an adult, so make sure you get enough calcium now to have strong bones later on. Milk, yogurt, cheese, and, well, milk all have calcium in them. Dark green veggies like broccoli and spinach also have calcium, as do some other foods like salmon.

5. What if a year has gone by and I haven't grown or gained weight?

It takes time to get bigger and gain weight, and it doesn't always happen as quickly or evenly as we'd like. Some people grow quickly at first, then slowly for a while, and then quickly again. Even though it doesn't look like it, you might be growing because your friends are growing faster than you are. But your body is working!

6. How come my hips get big?

During puberty, a girl adds weight because her hormones rise. The shape of her body also changes. Her breasts get bigger and her hips and legs get wider. Girls usually gain weight around their hips and legs. This fat makes their bodies ready for when they might get pregnant.

7. Friends tell me I need a bra, but I'm too shy to ask for one. What should I do?

Like many other people, you probably feel embarrassed sometimes asking for a bra. You haven't had many chances to ask for a bra before, and getting breasts is also something new for you. Friends telling someone to buy a bra doesn't mean they need to. If you think a bra would help support your breasts, then buy one.

8. Why do I have stretch marks on my breasts?

Stretch marks appear on your body where your skin has grown quickly or where you've gained weight quickly. The 'marks' are where different layers of skin can show up because the skin is moving.

9. I have a question about the hair. Does it hurt when it grows?

It's okay for hair to grow. Since your hair doesn't have any nerves, the pain-sensing threads that connect to our brains — cutting your head hair doesn't hurt either.

10. Can you tell me if the period lasts 4-7 days or 47 days?

In most cases, the fluid that leaves your body lasts between 4 and 7 days and nights. However, some women have periods that last a few days more or less.

11. Do you still have changes in mood as an adult?

Yes! We all have feelings that change as the day or event goes on. Adults often don't act on as many thoughts as younger people do because their brains have been wired for longer and have had more experiences. So, even though older people feel a lot of different feelings every day, we don't always act on them.

Printed in Great Britain
by Amazon

48152783R00096